NICK WARBURTON was a pr
teacher for several years be
become a writer. He has wr
plays for the stage and television, including
Conversation from the Engine Room, which
won the 1985 BBC/Radio Times Drama
Award. He has also written several children's
books, among which is *The Battle of Baked
Bean Alley* (Walker, 1992), and his short
stories have been broadcast on BBC Radios
3, 4 and 5. He lives in Cambridge with his
wife and son.

NORMAL NESBITT

NICK WARBURTON

WALKER BOOKS
LONDON

First published 1992 by Walker Books Ltd
87 Vauxhall Walk, London SE11 5HJ

Text © 1992 Nick Warburton
Cover illustration © 1992 Martin Chatterton

This book has been typeset in 11/13pt Sabon

Printed and bound in Great Britain by
Richard Clay Ltd, Bungay, Suffolk

British Library Cataloguing in Publication Data
A catalogue record for this book is
available from the British Library.

ISBN 0-7445-2440-7

For my mother and father

*Nick Warburton would like to thank
the West Sussex Institute of Higher Education
for their help and support during 1991–2*

Nesbitt: **The First Domino**

I've traced it back and this is how it began. You make one stupid decision and it's like knocking down the first domino: you can't do much about the rest. They just keep falling.

There were three keen types jogging round the school field. You know what I mean by keen types: always ready to have a go. It didn't matter what. Joining clubs, Saturday jobs, whatever. In this case it was running round the field. They were in training, according to their leader, Metson, but he was doubly keen. The handsome sort who's a size too big for his jacket and who uses powerful soap. Metson was especially keen on his strong jaw line, which he was always studying in reflections, and his torso. He had a great torso; so he kept telling us. He took it with him wherever he went. I sort of liked him for it. (Not his torso, I should say. Just the fact that he was so keen on it. I mean, I can admire keenness without being keen myself.)

It was a warm day to be running, especially running in circles, so Trevor Baines and I were sitting on the grass, watching.

"Look at them, Noddy," Brains said after a while. "How do they make you feel?"

"Glad to be sitting down," I said.

"No, seriously. They're out there doing something and we're just sitting here on our bums. As usual. It makes me feel like a slob."

"I don't mind being a slob. Some of my best friends are slobs."

"Well, I'm not going to be one of them. Come on."

And he stood up and made off in the direction of the joggers. At first I thought this was a joke. Brains was not the jogging type. In fact, he was hardly even the moving type. He put more effort into getting out of Games than he ever did on those rare occasions when he was forced to take part. And here he was, *choosing* to go and jog. At lunch time.

He tagged on behind Metson and the others and I still thought it was a joke.

"Come on, Noddy," he called to me. "Let's move. Let's *do* something for a change."

And I thought, well, why not? What harm can it do?

So I hauled myself up and joined in. I could've stayed where I was and watched. I *should've* stayed where I was. I know Brains. I know what it usually means when you agree to his ideas. It's usually a mistake. This time, though, it was more than just a mistake.

It was the first domino.

Brains: *The Importance of Getting Off Your Bum Now and Then*

The thing about Nesbitt is that he's happy to let things happen. I'm not like that. The sight of Metson running was like a spur to me. I suddenly saw a lifetime of slobbishness ahead. There's two sorts of people, I thought. Those who get off their bums and do things, and those who slob around and watch. Watch telly, watch the others doing things, watch the grass growing. And what was I doing? Sitting on the grass, watching. So of course I joined in. It was my decision. Nesbitt was capable of making up his own mind. He can't say I forced him to run.

Anyway, it wasn't that much of a disaster. I don't know why he made such a big thing of it. After all, whatever else he became – and that wasn't my fault either – he certainly didn't become a slob. He ought to be grateful to me for that.

At the time, Nesbitt had just stopped being new. If you're new to a place you either stick out like a lighthouse on a boating lake, or you're quiet and you merge into the background. Nesbitt was the quiet sort. A proper merger. He joined the school at the beginning of term and I showed him the ropes. Well, someone had to. He had no idea which end was which. When someone's new you make allowances. They forget their way, keep making mistakes and so on. They really need someone around who knows how many beans make five. Nesbitt was lucky I took him on.

Well, we tagged along behind the others and

jogged round the field for a bit, and it all seemed to be OK. I mean, I was hardly sweating, so I thought we ought to put a bit more effort into it.

"OK," I said. "Flat out for the last lap."

"What?" said Noddy, giving me a sideways glance.

"Flat out. See who's first back."

"What for?"

"Oh, come on, Noddy. Put some effort into it for once in your life."

That was Noddy's trouble. He was happy enough to jog along with the crowd. He actually *liked* merging in with the background. The thing is, though, you can't stay new all your life. People won't always make allowances and forget who you are. After a month you've got to make your mark, haven't you?

That's what I was doing, then. Helping him to make his mark.

Minutes of the First Meeting of the Lower School Athletics Appreciation Society

Those present: Miranda de Beere (Chair), Francis Whale (Secretary), J. Corduroy, S. James (Ordinary Members). The aims of the group were discussed. S. James suggested "to appreciate Athletics in the School". F. Whale said we could do that at home. M. de Beere suggested "to *actively* appreciate Athletics in the School". F. Whale said that was bad English, but he was shouted down. Suggestion passed. Agreed that we should attend Upper School training sessions as observers. J. Corduroy said that Malcolm Metson was training at lunch times on the field and we should observe him. M. de Beere agreed. (Metson is a real man!) Rude comments from F. Whale noted and then ignored. Meeting adjourned so we could go straight out to the school field to see what was going on.

(M. de B.)

Nesbitt: **Not First and Not Last**

Trevor Baines had the perfect build for a middle-distance runner: no spare weight and not much height, a bit like a whippet. But that was deceptive. Even after a couple of minutes' jogging he was wheezing and his hair was stuck to his forehead with sweat. He couldn't run. In fact there wasn't much that he could do. Physical or mental. No coincidence that people called him Brains, I suppose. When he came up with his daft idea of making a race of it, Metson was dead keen. Well, of course he was.

"Great," he said. "Let's go for it."

So we did. There wasn't much else we could do once he'd got hold of the idea. We jogged level and then, at a shout from Metson, went belting round the last lap, trying to beat each other.

This is stupid, I thought as we pounded over the grass. Metson's bound to win. He was third in the district in last year's Halliwell Bowl, according to Brains, and that was a proper cross-country. A

11

numbered vests job. I couldn't see the point of jogging ourselves silly behind a souped-up torso, just to be humiliated.

Besides, something else occurred to me: we had Run and Swim in the afternoon. At least, I thought we had. Being new, I wasn't sure. They have this weird system of counting the days at this place. Each week lasts a week and a half, in order to fit the timetable in. You have to have a pass in Maths just to know where you're supposed to be. In fact, for my first three weeks at the school I had the impression that time was standing still and my growth rate had slowed down. Well, I still didn't understand it properly, but I reckoned that if this was day seven in week three, we had Run and Swim. And we were going to be knackered before we even started.

Holloway wasn't going to like that. He'd make life even more difficult for us than usual. ("Put some guts into it, you limp rags! When I was your age I could hop faster than that!" And so on and on. When he was our age, Holloway must have been such a perfect specimen I'm surprised no one had him stuffed. Hunk Holloway was another bloke with a torso.)

Still, I didn't want to be beaten, especially by Brains, so I did my best. Pumped the old arms and legs for all I was worth.

Metson was soon metres ahead of the rest of us.

"And it's Metson!" we heard him shouting in the distance as he streaked over the line, leading with his jaw and punching the air in triumph. "Metson, well ahead of the field and still looking very fresh. What a fantastic prospect this lad is!"

And he meant it, although he was a bit ashamed of it when the race was over.

"I'm not being boastful, Norbert," he explained. "I just happen to think I can run. I mean, I've got potential."

"Great," I said.

I'd lumbered in third – two ahead and two behind me – and collapsed in a heap with pains in my chest so there wasn't much else I could say. I couldn't even tell him my name wasn't Norbert. Brains was last. He just about managed to crawl over the line and slump down next to me. If it had been a real race at a real meeting they'd have wrapped him in one of those cooking-foil blankets and carried him off on a stretcher.

"That was a bit of a stupid suggestion, wasn't it?" I told him.

He lay on his back sucking in air and didn't answer.

"You might've guessed Metson would walk it. He won't let us forget this, you know."

Brains pulled himself on to his elbows and tried to speak. All that came out was a sort of bubbly gasp. We watched Metson doing press-ups for a while.

"Anyway," I said. "You knew you'd come last."

"No, I didn't," he managed to say. "I thought I was in with a chance."

"Well, *I* knew you'd come last. You always come last."

"And I knew you'd come third," he wheezed, falling back on the grass and staring at the sky.

"Third? What's wrong with that?"

"Nothing," said Brains. "I just knew that's where you'd come, that's all."

He knew I'd come third? So what? Coming third was better than coming last. Wasn't it? Maybe he was delirious with the effort of getting his weedy body round that last lap and didn't really know what he was saying. But he made it sound like an insult. As if coming third *was* worse than coming last.

Brains: *It's Not Always Winning That Counts*

What really drained me was the long grass. I couldn't help noticing that the grass just happened to be longest where I was running. I mean, you'd never get conditions like that on a real track. It drags your legs back. None of the others had this problem. To them it was just a matter of making a bit of a dash for the line. Simple. Whereas I'd gone through the pain barrier before we'd even reached the final stretch. Not that I gave up. You just don't do that. That's not what running is about. You see, I wasn't just running against Metson and the others. I was running against the pain that was racking my own body. It was a kind of triumph of sheer bloody iron will that I crossed the line at all. Nesbitt didn't have much sympathy, though. He thinks getting out of bed in the mornings is going through the pain barrier. Pathetic, really. I mean, I *showed* him the long grass and he simply failed to see it.

"You knew you'd come last," he said smugly.

Well, I knew he'd come in the middle. Middle of the road, that's Nesbitt. It seems to me that coming only a fraction behind the others with the burden of pain I had on my shoulders is a little better than plodding in a very ordinary third.

(I was going to tell him about my tetanus booster. I only had it done a week or so ago and it really drains you, you know. But I didn't bother to mention it in the end. *I* know how well I did. That's what counts.)

Minutes of the Second Meeting of the L.S.A.A.S.

Observations on training session: after a bit of jogging round, M. Metson organized a race which he won by miles. Naturally. It was a pretty poor turn-out, though. A couple of weeds from the Upper School were talked into the race by M.M. but they were useless. One was Brains, Chief Wimp of the U.S., and the other some new bloke nobody had seen before. (No one could remember his name either.) J. Corduroy said she had to leave early to watch some puerile soap on TV. Not much commitment there.

(M. de B.)

"Put your backs into it, you two! You look as if you're ambling round the corner to buy a paper!"

"We're saving ourselves, sir," said Brains.

Hunk Holloway stood with his hands on his hips, his whistle still gripped in his teeth. Glowing with health. You see a lot of Hunk Holloways on the covers of Mills and Boon romances. Although he was some distance off, I could tell that he was narrowing his eyes. He dropped the whistle from his mouth and came loping easily down the field towards us.

"What was that, Baines?"

"I said we're saving ourselves, sir."

"What for? The pension?"

"No, I mean we're pacing ourselves; trying to judge things..."

"Or, to put it another way, ambling."

I didn't argue. I didn't feel up to it. My muscles were like warm toffee. It felt as if I only had one per limb. Besides, it was never a good idea to argue with Hunk. He was beaming his white teeth at us now and that wasn't a good sign.

"OK, lads," he said. "Stop running."

Which was supposed to be a joke, because we'd already slowed to a walk when we saw him coming. He moved in between us, lowering his voice and draping an arm over our shoulders.

"You do realize," he said, "that your bodies, such as they are, have reached a very important stage of their development?"

We didn't answer but, then, we weren't meant to.

16

"What you make of them now will influence what they will be like in twenty years' time. I don't ask you to run so that we can keep the school grass down, you know. I ask you to run so that, when you reach manhood, you will be fit and ready for anything. The way you're going on now, you'll only be fit to shuffle backwards and forwards between your TV and your armchair."

"We've got a remote control, sir," said Brains.

"Not funny, Baines," said Hunk, tightening his grip on our collar bones. Mine as well as Brains', even though I hadn't said a word.

"At some point I want you to stand in front of a mirror and look at your weedy frame and your pasty flesh and ask yourself, 'Is this what I really want to look like when there's a chance I could look a bit more like Mr Holloway?'"

A thudding of feet behind us signalled the approach of Metson and two or three other athletic types. They pounded by in a whirl of arms and legs and we moved aside to watch. Hunk was deeply impressed.

"Look at that," he said. "That is what I call making the most of things. And that is what I want to see you doing. Now, get moving."

He gave us a shove in the back and we trotted off after the others.

"Come on! Faster! Change gear, Niblett."

I changed gear, but I don't think he noticed. I couldn't help wondering whether life would be easier if I got a torso too. Maybe I could save up for one.

Brains: *Facing Up to Yourself*

I did what he said. I looked at myself in the mirror in the changing rooms. Just a quick look; too many nosy types around for anything else. It wasn't that bad. I reckon he was really meaning Noddy, who's a bit flabbier than me. I'm what you might call tightly constructed. Not much spare flesh, but all very nicely put together. So I've been told. The only possible criticism I could make of my body is that it is not bulging with muscles. This isn't a serious problem, though. A lot of girls like a small, neat frame.

Last year at Clacton I met this girl called Emma. Very nice. Dark hair and blue eyes, which is a killing combination. She didn't seem to mind a small, neat frame. I was by the pool when I first saw her. We talked. It was so easy it was almost as if I'd known her for years. The weather was rotten and we played table-tennis. Then at the end of the week there was a disco...

Anyway, the point is, there's nothing much wrong with my body. Only, no one's perfect, are they? I mean, there *is* room for some improvement and if I could just put an extra layer of muscle over what I've already got, well, I'd probably have to beat them off with a stick.

I thought I might try some exercises. A few press-ups, maybe. Always improve, that's my motto. Always look for ways to better yourself.

Nesbitt: *An Encounter With Madge*

I was on my way to the library and it was so hot
that I'd taken my jacket off. A heinous crime at this
place, though I'd forgotten that for the moment.
You can be drunk and disorderly in a dinner queue
and they'll turn a blind eye, but just let them catch
you without your jacket on and you're really for it.

The corridor, I suddenly noticed, was empty. Or
almost empty. Just me and our noble Head, who
had appeared out of nowhere and was glaring at
me. Alsopp, R.A., M.A. (Cantab), a suit and
document case man. In control of things. He called
himself hard but fair. ("You play fair by me, lad,
and I'll most certainly play fair by you.") We called
him Madge.

"You! Where do you think you're going?"
Alsopp barked.

He made me jump and I didn't answer at once.
I started struggling into my jacket. It was a kind of
reflex action.

"And where did you get that?" he said, moving
towards me.

He eyed the jacket and leaned over me with a
sour look on his face.

"Well?"

"In town, sir," I said. "Carter's."

"Don't try and be funny with me, boy. You're
from St Peter's, aren't you?"

"St Peter's?"

"And you needn't try any of your innocent
expressions on me. I've been around far too long
for that kind of thing. You St Peter's lot think you

can come in here in broad daylight and disrupt the workings of the school..."

"I'm not from St Peter's, sir," I managed to say. "I'm from here."

"No, you're not."

"I am, sir. I'm on my way to the..."

"What's your name?"

"Nesbitt. Gordon Nesbitt."

"I don't believe you. Let me tell you, we have almost two thousand pupils here. I know them all. Every face and name. It's my job and I pride myself on doing my job well. So don't try and tell me you're from here because I *know* you're not."

And he started bundling me towards the exit. We were halfway to the main gate before I could convince him I was one of his and not St Peter's. I didn't even know where St Peter's was. He settled for tearing me off a strip for not wearing my jacket and stalked back to his room. No apologies. You don't get apologies from Madge. Whatever you've done he makes you feel you're in the wrong. Even when you've done nothing.

Alsopp: *Memo to Self*

Almost ejected one of my own students this afternoon. A strange occurrence. Had no idea who he was. Slightly worrying. Have always taken a great deal of trouble to acquaint myself with all my students; studied photographs, records and what have you. This is the first one to slip through the net. He was rather an unexceptional specimen, reasonably new to the school. He wasn't wearing his jacket and I assumed he was one of the wide boys from St Peter's who seem to take such delight in infiltrating our establishment. Must look into this boy's case and get to know him better. The name is Niblick, so he says.

Nesbitt: **Caught in Time**

At the end of the afternoon I was waiting for Brains by the gates when Jackie Maugham took a photograph of me. It wasn't what I was expecting. I was lounging against a brick pillar and my mind was on nothing in particular. She looked as if she was going straight past, but she suddenly stopped and aimed the camera.

Click. Whirr.

"Here," I said. "What are you up to?"

"Don't get worked up," said Jackie. "It's only a photo."

"What do you want a photo of me for?"

"I don't want a photo of you. I want a photo of the gates. You just happened to be in the way."

Jackie's a strange girl. It didn't surprise me that she wanted a photo of a brick pillar, but I wasn't too pleased to be in it. It made me feel uncomfortable. I had the feeling my mouth had been hanging open and I'd been looking a bit thick.

"Why didn't you ask me to move, then?" I asked her.

"Because you're part of the scene, that's why."

Just then Brains came straggling across the

21

tarmac, dragging his bag behind him, his shirt half out and his hair looking like a pile of swept-up leaves.

"Why not take a picture of Brains?" I asked.

"No thanks," she said and moved off.

"What are you going to do with it?" I called after her.

"It's for my portfolio: scenes from school life."

"What?"

"A week in the life of the school with pictures of various parts of the building at different times of the day."

"I don't see the point."

"The school as it really is," explained Jackie, still walking away. "The highs and the lows of an average week. It's a project for Humanities."

I didn't ask her whether I was supposed to be a high or a low. I knew what she would've said.

"I shouldn't think you'd be either, would you?" Brains said as we walked home.

"Wouldn't I?"

"I shouldn't think so. You'd be about the middle somewhere, wouldn't you?"

Which reminded me of our conversation at lunch; about me coming third in the race against Metson. It gave me the chance to ask him what he meant by it.

"I don't know. I wasn't thinking. I just guessed you'd come somewhere in the middle, I suppose."

"In the middle?"

"Yes. About average."

"Average?"

"Yes. Why?"

"I don't know. I wondered what you were getting at, that's all."

Brains said he wasn't getting at anything – which was probably true – and we dropped the subject. Well, we stopped talking about it. It was still floating round in my head somewhere and I couldn't quite shake it out.

Brains: *A Helping Hand for Nesbitt*

The press-ups were a good idea. Five before dinner and five last thing. Actually, I only managed four tonight. Dad was passing by on the landing and I had to pretend I was looking for something under the bed. Still, no problem. I'll do six tomorrow.

They're very invigorating. Funnily enough, you feel more energetic after a few press-ups than you did before; as if you're tingling with energy. Ready for anything.

Poor old Noddy looked really put out by having his picture taken. This is probably a throwback to his primitive past. It's a well-known fact that primitive people think you've got their soul when you take their picture. I don't suppose he realizes it, but I expect that's what's getting to Noddy. I told him Jackie probably wanted it for a pin-up, so she could stick it on her bedroom wall and drool over it. Which is quite a funny thought. I mean, if Jackie wanted a pin-up she wouldn't go for Nesbitt, would she? She's more likely to go for someone like Metson. Thick but macho.

The idea of Jackie taking glamour pics is not a

bad one, actually. An interesting reversal of roles. In a week or two she could take me. Take pictures, I mean. I wouldn't mind. I might even suggest it. She could take a few of me and, well, I could take a few of her. No one could say that was sexist or anything.

But it's not really Noddy's scene. He couldn't handle it because he gets embarrassed too easily. He's a funny bloke. A bit old-fashioned and awkward. He leans on me a lot. Being that much more experienced in what you might call street culture, I can prevent him making too much of a prat of himself. You know where you are with Noddy, though. He's reliable. He doesn't let you down. He's the only bloke I know who hasn't got something weird about him.

Nesbitt: *A Dog's Best Friend*

I should explain about Colin. He's the family dog. We have two parents, two boys (me and Stuart, who is eleven and interested in toy cars and nothing else) and Jeanette. She's a sort of sister; wants to be an actress, she says. She probably will be too. She's always flouncing about, pretending to be what she isn't, with a queue of drooling yobbos behind her. Mum had Jeanette when she was married to her first husband. He cleared off – shortly after Jeanette was born, which might've had something to do with it – and Mum married my dad. Then along came me and Stuart. Which brings us to Colin.

As I said, he's our dog. He doesn't actually belong to anyone in particular – he's not a belonging sort of dog. But I do most of the feeding and walking, and I get on with him best. Most days I take him for a walk by the river. On decent days we go to the park. He's a floppy Labrador with a golden coat and an intelligent face. He likes the park. I think he enjoys watching passers-by best, but he does a bit of lolloping over the grass for the sticks I throw for him. Only as a favour to me, I think. He's kind-hearted like that. And a good listener.

If there's anything I can't talk to Brains about, I tell Colin. I know how that sounds – as if I've a screw loose somewhere – but I find it helpful. You need *someone* to talk to these days. Anyway, for a dog he gives pretty good advice. I've never really thought about it before, but he's probably more intelligent than Brains. He certainly doesn't do so many stupid things.

That evening after school was still warm so we went to the park.

"Holloway got my name wrong again," I said to Colin. "And Madge didn't even know who I was."

"Well," he said, "it's because you're new, isn't it?"

"I don't know. I've been there over a month. I can't go on being new."

"That's true."

"Anyway, I don't feel like flogging myself round a running track for someone who calls me Niblett."

Colin stopped walking, yawned and sat down on the grass.

"You shouldn't let that worry you," he said. "If you're going to run you should run for the sake of running, not because Hunk wants you to run."

"I suppose so."

"Besides, they're always calling you Nisbett or Nosbert, or George instead of Gordon..."

"I know, and I get fed up with it sometimes. Gordon Nesbitt isn't that hard to remember, is it?"

"I expect they muddle other people's names as well, don't they?" suggested Colin.

"Not that I've noticed. I mean, no one ever makes a mistake over Baines' name."

"No, they wouldn't. Baines is a fairly unusual bloke."

"And I'm not, I suppose."

"I didn't say that, Gordon."

And, of course, he hadn't said that. But it got me thinking.

As Colin and I were on our way out of the park we almost tripped over Brains, who was stretched out on a bench, sunbathing. He didn't seem to mind displaying his spindly body to the public. I don't think they cared much for it, though. Two old ladies with sticks walked by and I saw them turn their heads away and mutter to each other. If it had been Metson they'd've hung around.

Anyway, we joined him. Colin settled down with his head on his paws, paying close attention to a man who was rowing a couple of kids on the boating lake. I closed my eyes and felt the heat on my face as I listened to the voices of the children, distant and small, drifting over the water. No one spoke for some time. I think I was beginning to doze off when Brains suddenly came to life and shook my knee.

"Noddy, quick!"

"What? What is it?"

"Look who's coming!"

I struggled to a sitting position and looked up the path. I could see nothing but swirling red blotches of light and an empty path. On one side were the flowerbeds and on the other the lake. The boat had gone, so that was empty too.

"The other way," hissed Brains.

Blinking hard, I twisted round. The path led into a small wood in that direction and I could see that someone was walking towards us in the shadow of the trees. A girl. Mottled sunlight moved all around her, making flickering patterns over her hair, and it was hard to make her out properly. I didn't think that I knew her. Colin had already seen her and was watching her carefully with his head up.

"Who is it?"

"Through the trees, coming this way," Brains said, not very helpfully.

"Yes, I see her. Who is it?"

"Who is it? You mean you don't know?"

The girl came out of the shadows. Her hair was so fair that it was almost white in the sunlight. I knew I'd never seen her before.

"Of course I don't know," I whispered. "Who is it?"

"That, my dear boy," Brains said knowingly, "is the new girl in Holloway's form. The Dumb Blonde."

Brains: *Getting to the Facts*

What else could you call her but the Dumb Blonde? Very blonde and most of the time pretty silent. Pretty and silent, let's be honest. Not dark hair and blue eyes, but all the same not bad either. Not bad at all. I was surprised that Noddy hadn't noticed her before. Although, now I come to think about it, I wasn't that surprised. He's always been a bit slow off the mark.

I found out the essential details – some of them, anyway – half an hour after she'd turned up at school. I make it my business to know about people. In fact, I've got a very good nose for essential details.

Her real name was Claire Brooks and she'd come from Devon, according to my sources. Her mother was some kind of doctor. I didn't know anything about her father. Not yet, anyway. There was something haughty about her; something that made you think twice before you tried talking to her. It was the sort of air that put Noddy off completely. When I first pointed her out to him I could see that look in his eyes. Like a rabbit about to go bouncing off down its hole.

She walked past us and turned her head, very slightly, to look at the lake. Or rather, not to look at Noddy and me. Very superior. I would probably have called her over, but I sensed that it would have made Noddy squirm. So I let it pass. Actually, I think she just didn't want to notice us. That's the impression I got. Haughty and silent. So, as I said, the Dumb Blonde seemed to be the right name.

And she was new, which meant that Nesbitt couldn't claim to be new any more.

The next time we saw her was at lunch on the following day. We were back on the field, but this time we weren't jogging. Noddy wasn't having any more of that.

"Today we're going to watch, OK?" he said. "I was nearly done for yesterday."

Metson was out there, though, flinging his arms about and going into sudden bursts of running on the spot as if he was trying to knee himself in the mouth.

"Come on, lads," he called to us. "Let's have another race."

He was tired of racing against himself and wanted someone to beat. I was game, but Noddy deliberately took no notice. I don't think he was up to running twice in one week. Also, I could see he was worried that Jackie was out there too, adding to her collection of interesting school pictures. I should imagine he didn't want her to take any more pictures of him, especially if he was red in the face and flat on his back.

Metson noticed Jackie and tried to persuade her to get a shot of his pectorals, as he put it. She ignored him and took a photograph of his trainers instead. Then another, so it looked to us, straight down at the grass. So maybe I was wrong about her wanting to get pictures of macho types. She wasn't into pics of blokes; she was into grass and footwear. Very peculiar. I wonder what she thinks about at night.

After a while Metson managed to talk a few more joggers into accompanying him round the track. Mostly younger ones like Miranda de Beere and Jo Corduroy, who'd been lying on their bellies gawping at him for ages.

"Like to join in, girls?" (Swoon, swoon.)

None of them came up as far as his shoulder. They'd only got about halfway round when the Dumb Blonde appeared in a tracksuit and started to limber up, which was quite a spectacle. She did the same sorts of things as Metson, but she didn't do them so furiously. You might say, if you had a way with words, that her movements were lithe and graceful. And such breasts. They were more or less perfect. I'm not being puerile here. If I didn't mention them I'd be dishonest. They were a feature.

I always think it's unnatural the way people avoid mentioning them. Oh yes, a lovely girl. Lovely eyes, lovely hair and so on. Breasts? Well, they claim, actually, I didn't notice. Who are they trying to kid? If a girl's got nice breasts why not simply say so? I mean, it doesn't make you a monster, or sick or anything, does it?

Anyway, Metson noticed her as he swept ahead of his little group of disciples.

"Fancy joining us?" he called out to her.

She didn't say anything, but shielded her eyes against the sun and peered at Metson for a while before running down to tag on with the rest of them. We watched them jog round for a couple of laps, Metson leading the way, the younger ones bobbing behind him and the Dumb Blonde at the back. After a while they came to a stop and Metson started to organize them into a line.

"Oh, no. He's at it again," said Noddy. "He's

getting them to run another race. I blame you for this, Brains."

"Why me?"

"Because you put the idea into his head."

"I don't see why it should bother you."

"It's the thought of all that energy wasted, chasing Metson..."

The runners were coming up the slope towards us and Metson was already pulling away from the rest. Enjoying himself. His feet came thumping past our faces as he swung round the bend. But just as we turned our heads to follow the progress of Metson's muscular bum towards the finish, the Dumb Blonde came swishing past us too. We hardly heard her feet hit the ground, but the breeze of her passing brushed against our faces. She caught Metson as he was about to cruise over the line and give his usual punch to the air for victory. You could tell that he hadn't heard her coming by the way his head jerked as she went by.

"See that?" I said in a hushed voice. "She beat him."

Metson did his best to be good about it.

"She's very light on her feet," he said as we walked back into school. "Which is a good sign. She runs well."

"You didn't hear her coming?" Nesbitt asked.

"No, I didn't. She caught me on the hop a bit."

"You'd beat her if you ran again, though," I urged, stirring Metson up a bit. And a man whose pride has been stung is not hard to stir up.

"Who knows?" said Metson. "I'd run it differently, of course, but, well ... she *is* good."

The girl herself came by just then, swinging her trainers by their laces, looking hard ahead of her so as not to catch anyone's eye.

"Well run," said Noddy. A brave move for him. Only two words, but for Nesbitt it was as good as a speech.

She started slightly and smiled by way of an answer. A very quick smile, on then off.

"You should have a rematch," I called out to her. "Metson thinks it wasn't a true test."

"I didn't say that..." said Metson, but his protests trailed away to nothing because the girl broke into a trot and left us behind. Again without a word.

She ran up the steps into the main corridor, where Hunk Holloway was sheepdogging people in. He must've been there long enough to have seen the race because he drew her to one side before she could slip by. I could imagine what he was saying to her.

"Nice run, lass. What I like to see. Have you thought about joining my training sessions?"

The sort of thing he said to the favoured few from time to time. So they claimed. He'd never spoken to Nesbitt or me like that. Not blonde enough and not pretty enough, I suppose.

Minutes of the Third
Meeting of the L.S.A.A.S.

The Chair, Secretary and other members of the Association were invited to take part in a race with Metson. Two members accepted this challenge and two (both male) chickened out. The race was won by Claire Brooks, the new girl. F. Whale says this means that Metson is not as good as he's cracked up to be, but I reckon it means something else. A bright future for school Athletics. Maybe Metson was being a gentleman and allowing her to win, but, even so, she's good and we'll have to watch her. Two members left the meeting early again. They didn't say why this time. F. Whale said he thinks it's because the L.S.A.A.S. has become boring. M. de Beere said, well, nothing's changed. We're doing what we said we'd do. He said, that's right – it was boring from the start. The Chair suggested we should take more interest in other things. The Secretary said, like what? We agreed to think about it and report back.

(M. de B.)

Nesbitt: A View of the Race
(and the Dumb Blonde)

You had to be impressed by that race. She looked born to run. And she didn't gasp for breath or pull faces like most runners, either. I bet she didn't even sweat. Or perspire – she wouldn't call it sweating.

No great surprise that Holloway should show so

much interest in the girl. He liked winners. I suppose that's why he had no time for Brains and me. He couldn't even get my name right so he wasn't going to want me out there on his training sessions. Not that I was interested. And he wouldn't want Brains out there, either, except as a piece of spare elastic to keep his shorts up.

But the Dumb Blonde was obviously a different matter. It was odd, though, that nobody had said anything about her looks. (Not to me, anyway.) Because she was pretty. Very pretty. Normally it was the sort of thing someone would comment on, especially someone like Brains, who has an unhealthy obsession with looks and, in particular, with breasts. (It hadn't occurred to me before, but this was the one thing that Brains and Metson had in common, this interest in breasts. The difference being that Metson was only interested in his own.)

Of course, I didn't say anything about the Dumb Blonde's looks myself, so maybe everyone was thinking it and waiting for someone else to make the first comment. I don't know.

Brains: *A Theory of Equality*

As far as I know, this theory has never been set out before. It's a case of original thought which I've built up over the last year or so.

The Dumb Blonde was a good runner, there's no doubt about it. It was her redeeming feature. That's the way I see it, anyway. Some people are clever, some are strong, some are good at art, and so on and so forth. Everyone has something. It all balances out. She was dumb but she could run.

It's a matter of talent. Talent and character. You have one or you have the other or you have a little bit of both. You either get "A" for talent and "E" for character, or you get "A" for character and "E" for talent. Or, of course, you get "C" for both. Which is probably where Noddy comes in. I explained all this to him in the library.

"Me?" he said. "Why?"

"Because you're a bit of both."

This wasn't easy for Nesbitt to grasp. To put it simply, the really talented people are usually swines. Can't get on with other people. Like Mozart. Wrote good music but he was a complete plonker when it came to socializing. No one liked him much at all. But even this wasn't quite simple enough for friend Noddy. Something or other had put him in an awkward mood.

"How do you know?" he asked.

"What?"

"How do you know Mozart was a plonker?"

"It's a well-known fact."

"I'm not so sure."

"Come off it, Nesbitt. What do you know about Mozart?"

"I know a bit."

"Exactly. You know a bit, but not much."

"Well, quite a bit, then."

"Oh, yes? Quite a bit? Tell me what he wrote, if you know quite a bit."

"Well..." I could see him casting around in his

mind for a piece of music. "He wrote Mozart's First ... and Mozart's Tenth..."

"Of course he did. No one else wrote them, did they? Anyway, you're getting off the point. We're talking about the Dumb Blonde here..."

"You mentioned Mozart."

"Will you let me get a word in, please, Noddy? The point is that Claire Brooks is a good enough runner to beat Metson, but she hasn't got much else going for her, has she?"

"What about looks?"

It surprised me to hear him say that. I didn't think he'd noticed her in that way. Well, he *had*, of course. You couldn't help noticing it. But it surprised me that he mentioned it. From the look on his face, it surprised him too.

"What do you mean, looks?" I asked.

"Well, she's not exactly ugly, is she?"

"Looks don't come into it. They're a matter of luck and, in any case, looks aren't going to count much after you're thirty, are they?"

"What about you, then?" he said.

"What about me?"

"You're not good at *anything*, are you?"

I knew what he was up to. This was a defensive reaction. He'd embarrassed himself by talking about Claire in that way and he was lashing out at the nearest target – me – to draw attention away from himself. It was obvious, really.

"You're good at talking cobblers," he said.

Still feeling sore, I could tell. I wasn't going to hold it against him, though. I'm bigger than that.

At this point, Metson breezed into the library

and strode over to us, bristling with fresh air and purpose.

"It's all fixed," he said, dumping his books on our table.

"What's all fixed?" asked Noddy.

"A re-run. With what's-her-name. That girl."

"Did you ask her?"

"No. Hunk arranged it. A proper race with just the two of us. He's going to act as judge and starter. Friday lunch time."

Alsopp: *Memo to Self*

No record of a Niblick anywhere. Made a few enquiries and discovered that there is a Nesbitt, though no one can confirm that this is the same lad I caught without his jacket. If it is I have to ask: Why did he give a false name? Perhaps there is more to this character than meets the eye. In order to put my mind at rest, have decided to call Nesbitt in for a chat.

Brains: *Introducing Toby*

Toby organizes most of the betting at school. In fact, I don't think he does much else. He's usually taking bets on something or other: the results of football and hockey matches, anything. Once he took a lot of bets on which member of staff would be the next to get a new car and there was almost a riot the morning Holloway came to school by taxi. Everyone thought he'd bought it and flew into a panic. Holloway usually cycles to school so he was one of the real outsiders.

Nesbitt and I ran into Toby on the way to school on the morning of the race.

"You taking bets on it?" I asked him.

"No, I'm not," said Toby.

"Why not?"

"Because it's not worth all the bother of setting odds and collecting bets. It's a two-horse race. Anything could happen."

"A football match is a two-horse race, isn't it?" Nesbitt asked. "And you take bets on them."

"It's not the same," said Toby. "I can only offer very short odds on Metson because he's almost bound to win. No one's going to take me up on it. And then supposing he falls over or something. It could happen. What becomes of the stake money then?"

"So you'd take bets if there were more runners?" I asked.

"Certainly. Much more interesting. Take the Halliwell Bowl, for instance. You're going to have about a hundred running in that, from all over the district. I could give you odds on Metson then. I could give you odds on someone from this school coming in the first three. I could give you odds on us taking the team trophy. I could give you odds on…"

We nipped round the side of the craft huts and left him muttering to himself. He could go on like that for ages if he wanted to. He reminded me a bit of a politician. Complete conviction about next to nothing.

"Ah well," I said. "It's going to be interesting, even without betting."

"Why, if Metson's going to win?"

"Well, the main reason is that the girl is going to be in the limelight. So far she hasn't spoken to anyone very much; kept herself to herself; seems a bit snooty. Now we're going to get a closer look at her under pressure."

"You make her sound like a rat in a maze," Noddy said.

What was this? Jumping to the lady's defence? Could friend Nesbitt be getting interested?

Nesbitt: Miss Cassidy: Something Different

"I think this week we're going to try something different in Humanities," Miss Cassidy told us.

There was nothing new in that. Miss Cassidy was always coming up with something different. As if she was afraid that the usual sort of Humanities would send us to sleep. Perhaps it would. We never found out, because we never did the usual sort. It was always something different. Miss Cassidy said she liked to approach things from unusual angles.

Brains said Colin was like that. I knew what he meant. Sometimes he would walk up behind you and make your knees buckle by butting his nose against your leg. (Colin, that is, not Brains.) He hardly ever barked so you hardly ever knew he was coming. Colin would have liked Humanities.

Anyway, the different thing we were going to try

this week was a survey of the school. It didn't sound *that* different. Not as different as some of her ideas. Like the one where we built a cardboard shack in the corner of her room and took turns to crouch in it. So we should experience the living conditions of certain South Americans. Actually, I took that one very seriously. When it was my turn for a spell in the shack I curled up inside and tried to think what it would be like to have next to nothing to my name.

At first it just seemed like a good idea. Very lazy and peaceful. Life like this could be quite pleasant. No Humanities for a start. No batty girls taking pictures of you with your mouth open. None of Jeanette's yobbish hangers-on pinching stuff out of the fridge. Then I thought, well, there wouldn't be a fridge either. Or black and white films on telly of a Saturday afternoon. Maybe even no Colin. I was feeling quite depressed when I crawled out. Even more so when I found that all the others had gone to lunch.

"The thing is," Miss Cassidy said with that enthusiastic, slightly barmy look on her face, "we're going to end up with a sort of multi-media presentation of school life, in here, by half term."

She paused and looked at us for a response, but we were waiting to hear how much work it would involve.

"Forget about exams for a change," she went on. "Forget about facts and figures. I'm looking for a co-operative effort. What I want us to create is a multi-faceted picture of the average school week for, say, an average pupil. OK? All sorts of approaches. Art work, music, if you like, interviews, computer profiles. Just fling yourselves into it."

Another pause. No one moved.

"It won't just be this form. Other groups will be making a contribution."

Well, that explained Jackie Maugham's screwball photographs. Wonderful, I thought. A multi-media exhibition with a blown-up photograph of Gordon Nesbitt leaning against a pillar with his mouth hanging open. That was going to do great things for my street cred.

"I thought you said forget about facts and figures," said Dawn.

"I did," said Miss Cassidy, looking surprised at this sudden sign of life in one of her pupils.

"Well, if it's about an average week and it uses computers, it seems to me that facts and figures are going to play a big part."

"Well, yes, Dawn. They'll play *a* part, certainly. I just meant forget about them in the exam context. Don't be inhibited by them."

"Only, it's a bit misleading," said Dawn.

"Yes, I'm sorry. Use facts and figures where they fit, of course. Is that the sort of contribution you'd like to make, Dawn?"

"Not particularly."

"Oh."

I shouldn't think Dawn wanted to make any contribution very much. Unless it was to moan about what everyone else did. Moaning was her strength; her talent, as Brains would say.

There was one thing Miss Cassidy introduced that was a bit different, and that was the dummy. She dragged this stuffed dummy, like a Guy Fawkes, into the room and sat it at her desk. It was dressed in school uniform, but it had no face. Must've taken her ages to make it.

"This," she said, "is going to be part of our display. Our average pupil. We'll build our results round him."

You could tell she was proud of it and thought it was a wonderful idea. Something *really* different; a solid, 3-D visual aid. Bound to generate a bit of interest. It didn't interest me all that much and, from the look of the others, it wasn't exactly sparking them off either.

"Take a good look at him," she said. "I want you to keep him in mind when you set about your various tasks. OK?"

I wasn't especially good at art or music or any of the other stuff on offer so I said I'd work on the computer side of things. I had a good reason for this. All the other activities might involve me in a lot of leg work, traipsing round the school. But the computer room had new padded chairs and was quite comfortable.

Predictably enough, Baines said he'd come in with me and a few others on the computers. He said he had a feeling he might just have a knack with them. I wasn't convinced – he was the only person I knew whose digital watch beeped at seventeen minutes past the hour. He'd been warned about it by those members of staff who were nervous and didn't like noise. Unfortunately he didn't know how to switch it off so he'd developed the habit of sitting with his wrist tucked in his armpit to deaden the sound. He wasn't going to be much help.

Minutes of the Final
Meeting of the L.S.A.A.S.

All members present. (Four.) Everyone's fed up with the Society so we're disbanding it. M. de Beere asked for alternative suggestions but no one had the wit to think of anything. She then said that if all people wanted to do was slope off and watch Australians with hair-styles in puerile soaps it was a dim lookout and very pathetic. People ought to belong to *some* sort of Society, just to prove they were alive. S. James said we still had funds and what were we going to do with them? (The first thing he's ever said, as far as I can remember.) J. Corduroy proposed that we spent half on Cokes and the other half should go on a bet on the Big Race. This was passed. We voted to see who we should bet on. Two said Claire and two said Metson. As M. de Beere was in the chair she had the casting vote and said the money should go on Claire. (Metson is a disappointment anyway.) Big argument about this, but as we were only talking about seventy-five pence it all seemed very childish. F. Whale said he had to go to buy some fish for his dinner so the voting went in favour of Claire by 2 to 1.

(M. de B.)

Nesbitt: A Premonition

Hunk took charge of the race as if it was some kind of Olympic final. He came dressed for activity, as he always did – vest and tracksuit bottoms – and

43

strutted about like a traffic warden in underwear. He even brought out a starting pistol.

"Keep well back, you people," he shouted to those who'd turned up to watch.

Not that there were very many. Miranda de Beere with a few cronies huddled by the finishing line. I'm not sure whether they came to watch Metson run – or whether they intended to support Claire, as a matter of principle. Solidarity. A lone female challenging the arrogant male. Just as likely that they'd come to see Holloway, I suppose. He had something of a following among some of the girls. I'm sure he knew it, too. Swanning about in his brilliant white vest.

"Two laps this time," he said to the runners. "That OK with you, Malcolm? Claire?"

Metson said that the longer distances probably favoured him – he was putting in a lot of training for the Halliwell Bowl which was over several miles – so he wouldn't mind making it one lap, to keep things as even as possible. You could see the way his mind was working. Do the decent thing, Metson. Don't win by too much. Claire just shrugged her acceptance, as if she was saying, "one lap, two laps, whatever you like." As if, in fact, she didn't much care.

"You can always tell," said Brains, nodding at the competitors as they jiggled about at the start, shaking their wrists. "Real athletes do that. It shows class. Everyone else stands about with their arms folded."

On an impulse I called out, "Good luck!" and they both looked across at me; both thinking I'd meant them. In fact, once I'd said it, I wasn't sure *who* I'd meant. Maybe just good luck in general. I'd said it without thinking. Metson gave me a smile and a casual wave, but Claire did nothing. She just looked a bit surprised.

And then I found this sudden but very sure thought in my head: she's going to do it. I reckoned I could see something in her eyes, in the blank way she looked back at me. Not really with us; her mind already in the race. And there was no doubt about it. She would win.

Holloway called them to the line and pointed the starting pistol in the air.

"What did you say?" I asked Brains quickly. "A pound?"

"What?"

"Did you say a pound against Metson winning?"

"Did I?"

"You did the other day. Are you still on?"

"You mean, you're going to put a pound on the Dumb Blonde?"

"If you like."

"OK. You're on."

And we slapped palms just as the gun went off.

Brains: *A Loss Leads to More Profit*

Metson went away like a train, determined to establish an early lead and then sit back on it and control the race from the front. Pretty shrewd, really. I'd've done the same. And Claire let him go.

I'm sure she actually let him get a twenty metre start. That made me think. She knows what she's up to, I thought.

For a lap and a half they ran round with that twenty metre gap between them. It was like an invisible bar preventing Metson getting any further ahead while, at the same time, stopping Claire closing on him. Then they came up the slope for the last time and Metson suddenly began to look as if he was running on sand. The gap between them just wasn't there any more. In fact, I don't think he slowed down at all. It just looked that way.

She passed him on the bend and that was that. She was still picking up speed as she crossed the line. Miranda de Beere and her little gang were springing up and down, clutching each other and squealing. They must've had money on her too. Anyway, they were certainly on her side now. Hunk Holloway smirked and looked as if he knew all along that this would be the result. And maybe he did. It was supposed to be his job to know about these things.

Of course, that was the end of my pound. A couple of minutes of whirring thighs and I was in debt. I coughed up with a good heart, though. I could see that it pleased Noddy and who am I to take these little pleasures away from a simple soul like him? Besides, it occurred to me that there just might be the chance of winning it back, with interest. Get some dosh on the Halliwell Bowl, I said to myself, and get it on quick while the odds are still worthwhile.

Minutes of the Fourth Meeting
of L.S.A.A.S. (Reformed)

Meeting called to share out winnings on the Big
Race. S. James, who'd said he'd see Toby and put
the money on, now tells us that Toby wasn't taking
bets anyway. So why didn't he mention this before?
Much heated discussion on this, and S. James left
early. We've still got seventy-five pence in funds
and, since I am not a criminal, we'll have to meet
again to decide what to do with it.

No one made any attempt to discuss Athletics
this time, apart from talking about the race. But it
was a good meeting. Maybe we should keep the
group and find a new purpose.

(M. de B.)

Nesbitt: *Trying to Forge Links*

Mum took Stuart into town to buy new shoes.

"Oh, Mum, do I have to?" he said as she yanked
him out of the door.

That was almost the only thing he said these
days, apart from making car noises and trying to
borrow money. Have a bath, Stuart. "Oh, Mum, do
I have to?" Go to bed, Stuart. "Oh, Mum, do I have
to?" If you told him to breathe he'd say the same
and probably suffocate just to be awkward.

Jeanette had dragged one of the yobbos off to go
skating, which was right up her street. Acting on ice.
She was quite good at it, too, and loved to make men
stop and look at her. Whizzing along backwards and

47

aiming her bum at the gaps between all the totterers. The yobbo of the moment was Justin. I don't know what he was like on ice, but he was pretty nifty with our fridge. I found a lump of cheese the other day with a bite taken out. You could see the teeth marks. Disgusting. I mean, you couldn't help wondering where else his mouth had been. I almost asked Jeanette but thought better of it.

So Colin and I had the house to ourselves for an hour. We watched a pathetic cartoon together. I could tell from the look on his face that Colin didn't think much of it. Garish colours and movements as stiff as cardboard. Sometimes the characters didn't move at all except for the odd blink, which had been put in by some computer to remind us that these were supposed to be real people. It was so bad you couldn't stop looking. The sort of thing Stuart loves because he's got no taste.

"The list of the Humanities Computer Group has gone up," I said casually, my eyes still fixed on the screen.

"For the Average School Week Project?" asked Colin.

"Yes. The Dumb Blonde's on it."

"The Dumb Blonde?"

"You know. The new girl. Claire."

"Ah, yes," said Colin, "the one you keep talking about."

Did I keep talking about her? I *mentioned* her, yes, but that was natural enough, wasn't it? After all, she was new and there was the race. That was worth a mention, surely. I didn't think I was making a specially big deal of it.

"You said she doesn't speak to people much," Colin said after a while. "Do people speak to her?"

"A bit, I suppose."

"Do you?"

"Only a couple of words. Not that they got any response."

"Then why not try talking to her? After all, she *is* pretty, Gordon..."

"How do you know?"

"I saw her in the park, remember?"

"Well, all right, she's pretty. But that's got nothing to do with it."

"No, of course not. I mean you should talk to her to put her at her ease. She is new and you know what that's like."

"True enough."

"So maybe she needs someone to be a bit friendly, Gordon. Have you thought about it like that?"

I hadn't, but I didn't tell him. It doesn't do to let a dog get too smug.

When I did try to speak to her, though, just to give her someone else to say hello to, I'm afraid I cocked it up.

Brains: *Nesbitt Tries to Play It Cool*

Noddy's attempt to chat up the Dumb Blonde made me realize what a long way he had to go.

We were in the computer room for the first group meeting of the Average School Week Project. (I was trying hard to control my tremblings of

49

excitement.) The aim was to feed in as many facts about the school population as we could gather. Names, dates of birth, height, and so on. Then we would be able to build a picture of the average pupil. We were given what they called "limited access" to certain records. Nothing too personal, I suppose that meant, which was a relief. (I could just imagine the screens spilling out info on some of my activities. "Baines, Trevor. Details of movements at Clacton during Summer Holidays...")

So Noddy sauntered up to the Dumb Blonde and patted the top of her computer.

"Do you understand about these things?" he asked her.

She turned and looked up at him as if he'd said something slightly insulting in a foreign language.

"Yes," she said, hooking a strand of yellow hair behind one ear. "Do you?"

OK, Nesbitt. Three mistakes in the first attempt. Let's take them in order.

One: you don't pretend to know about things if you're basically ignorant. You'll be found out sooner or later and you'll look an even bigger prat than you really are.

Two: don't simper. If you must look like some creep on a coffee advert, make sure the girl thinks you're doing it for a laugh. Never, never, *never* play it for real.

Three: if the girl does respond to this crass approach, don't blush.

I reckon he knew he'd mucked it up, because he gave up after that and crawled off to his own computer. Which he couldn't get started. Every

time he bashed the keyboard there was an embarrassing peep, as if the machine was smacking the
back of his hand. "No, Gordon. Don't touch me
there!" And all the time poor old Mr Cool was
practically shrinking away to nothing in his chair.
If it had gone on much longer he'd have disap-
peared completely. Oddly enough it was Claire who
put him out of his misery. There he was, bashing the
keys and dripping with sweat, when she leaned over
him with a sweet, sweet smile.

"It's quite simple, really," she said, deliberately
sounding like some playgroup leader. "You've left
the Shift Lock on."

That girl has a cruel streak. I should have
warned him. Blondes can be cruel. A dark-haired
girl would never do a thing like that.

Alsopp: *Memo to Self*

The Nesbitt problem. Wandered along to a class
Ron Peck was taking. Ron pointed Nesbitt out, but
the face meant nothing to me. Couldn't link it with
that encounter over the jacket at all. Perhaps it was
Nesbitt, perhaps not. Decided to box clever on this
one. Don't want to be accused of victimizing the
innocent, making mountains out of molehills etc.,
etc. Ron P. thinks that Nesbitt is friendly with
Trevor Baines. I know Baines. Of course. *So* –
perhaps I should have a few quiet words with him
first. Softly, softly, catchee monkey.

51

Nesbitt: *Why Am I a Mug?*

Monday lunch time: Brains took his tray and went weaving through the tables like a man with a mission. I should've realized that he was up to something. We passed a perfectly good, empty table right near the end of the queue. It's not like him – or me for that matter – to walk further than necessary.

"There's a table here," I said. "What's wrong with this?"

"I've got a plan, Gordon. Trust me," he said and forged on.

I couldn't see the harm in sitting where he wanted, so I followed. A mistake. "I've got a plan, Gordon." Ominous words from the mouth of someone like Brains. I really should've been suspicious. I just don't think quickly enough where Brains is concerned. He reached his destination and whipped the tray out behind him for me to return to the stack. Like a mug I did just that. As if I was his man-servant or something.

"You're a mug, Nesbitt," I told myself. "You know you're a mug. Why do you do it?"

It was only when I got back to him that I saw he'd plumped himself next to Claire. For a moment I hesitated, thinking I might move somewhere else. But that's exactly what's wrong with me. I hesitate and think and then it's too late.

"Great run," said Brains to Claire with a sickening smile. "On Friday, I mean."

She looked with suspicion from him to me, but said nothing. I concentrated on my plate, determined to say nothing either.

"You've obviously got talent," he told her.

I guessed that this was Brains trying to be cool – the wry smile, the nodding head, the knowing voice. He looked like a garden rake doing Terry Wogan impersonations. Leaning towards Claire, he lowered his voice and asked, "I wonder if anyone's mentioned the Halliwell Bowl to you?"

"Yes," she said. "Mr Holloway has."

"I'm not surprised. I'm not in the least surprised. You must have a great chance of taking the girls' section. Maybe even the whole race..."

"Well, I've entered. We'll have to see, won't we?"

"Mind you, it's a tough race. Some people don't even finish. It's not a good idea to go in unprepared."

"You're going in for it too, are you?" she asked. There was a hint of amusement in her voice and she glanced deliberately at Brains' pie and chips. Not the sort of stuff you pack away if you're in training.

"Oh no," said Brains. "My interest is in the tactical side of things. The logistics, the training, you know. I've found it's something I've got a knack for."

"Really?"

She was never going to buy all this. Even in the short time she'd been at the school she must've realized that the only thing Brains had a knack for was making a prat of himself. And, maybe, embarrassing his friends. He leaned further forward.

"I think I might be able to help you," he said.

Now he was reminding me of the coach in

Chariots of Fire, the one who punched a hole in his hat when his mate won a gold medal. In fact, I'm sure Brains reminded himself of that too. I'm sure he was playing that part. There was nothing for me to do but cringe. I had this horrible feeling that Claire was about to put him down and that the shock wave of shame and humiliation might splash all over me as well. But I couldn't do anything about it – he'd gone too far to be rescued now.

"You're fast," he ploughed on, "but I think you could be faster. I can give you another couple of metres."

"You think so?"

"That's over the short distance, of course. Over a course like the Halliwell Bowl, we're really talking about *hundreds* of metres."

"Are we?"

"At a rough estimate. I can't be sure till I've gone into it more thoroughly, of course."

This is it, I thought. This is where Brains gets the last forkful of her coleslaw in his face. I could hardly bring myself to watch. Out of the corner of my eye I saw her sweep her hair back and rest her chin on her hand. Letting him dig his own grave. Calmly allowing him to make an out and out plonker of himself, with all the finishing touches. It was cruel, really; far too calculating for my liking.

"And when could you do all this, Brains?"

Brains. She called him Brains. I could hardly believe it. The friendly touch before the killer blow.

"Lunch times are favourite," said Brains.

"OK," she said. "I'll see you out there in five minutes."

I was still flinching in anticipation of some kind of violence as she stood and collected up her plates. He was surprised too. I could tell by the way his voice dropped and lost all its cockiness.

"Great. Good. We'll be there."

"You'll both be coming, will you?" she asked and I could feel her looking directly at me.

"Not me," I said.

Brains was on his own as far as I was concerned. Nothing good was going to come of this. I could sense it and I wanted to be well out of the way. Preferably in comfortable surroundings.

"I promised someone I'd be in the computer room."

"Oh, of course," smiled Claire.

"I – er – wanted to take a look at a few statistics and – er..."

I don't know why I was explaining myself like that. Maybe I didn't want her to think I was staying away because of her.

"Well," she said as she left, "don't forget to release the Shift Lock, will you?"

Brains: *Probing Nesbitt's Emotions*

The press-ups were going pretty well. I was still keeping up a fairly punishing schedule: five in the morning and five at night. As well as toning me up it gave me an insight into the proper way to train. So I thought, how can I put this new skill to good use? The answer was easy. By offering my services to someone who needed them. Claire. Of course, the very thought put Noddy in a wild flap.

"Why?" he asked after I'd set the thing up.

"Well, why not?"

"I'll tell you why not," he said, tapping his fork on the table. "One: she's snooty. Two: you don't know anything about running. Three: there are better things to do. Four: she doesn't want anything to do with the likes of us..."

"She said yes."

"And five: you didn't tell me you were going to make a prat of yourself in front of her. 'Trust me,' you said and you went ahead."

"Honestly, Noddy, you're so negative. Here's a chance for us to do a bit of good for the school..."

"Not *us*, thank you very much."

"All right, me, then. But you'll regret it. When she starts getting a bit of fame and glory you'll be sorry you aren't on the team. Besides..."

"Besides what?"

"I quite like her."

"Like her? *Like* her?"

Well, of course I liked her. Who wouldn't? It was no good pretending to be amazed. He couldn't fool me.

So it was cards on the table time for Nesbitt. I had to make him face up to the fact that this was no ordinary bit of stuff and that he was fighting a passion for her in his dull breast.

"I like her and *you* like her. She's a looker, Noddy," I said, lowering my voice. "A real looker. And don't tell me you hadn't noticed, because you were the first to mention it."

"There's more to people than looks, Brains," he

56

said, and that was the end of the conversation. Snooty, he called her. I ask you. If anyone was sounding snooty it was him.

So off he toddled to play with the computers and I was left to put my plan into action by myself. I didn't mind. He would've cramped my style anyway. Needless to say he didn't really want to shut himself away in the computer room. He only said he was going there because he was scared. Scared of the Dumb Blonde. Is there any hope for a bloke like that, I wondered?

Nesbitt: Face to Face With Yourself

You get a good view of the field from the computer room. I'd forgotten that. I stood at one of the computers, put the disc in and brought the program on the screen. No trouble this time, I noticed. Why is it that I can only do things properly when there's no one about to see?

I turned, without really meaning to, and looked out of the window. I saw Brains and Claire talking earnestly. I sat down and swivelled round so I couldn't see them. Let them get on with it, I thought, and tried to concentrate on what I was doing.

I thought I'd feed in a few more figures, but I discovered that they'd all been done. So I began to play around, calling up a few lists to see what they looked like. Average height, for instance. Names began to roll down the screen – about twenty of them, all with the same height as the average we'd worked out earlier. One name stuck out: Nesbitt, G.

"Average height?" I said out loud. "That can't be right."

I'd always thought of myself as a bit taller than average. I was taller than Brains but, then, Brains was definitely shorter than average. It didn't worry me, though. Not at that stage.

I called up another list. Age, in years and months. The names rolled again and, again, there was mine. Nesbitt, G. Average age. I wasn't sure I liked that. It sounded a bit like middle-aged. Nesbitt, G., the middle-aged schoolboy. A kind of freak. It irked me, but, as I say, it didn't worry me too much. It should've done. Still, I had no way of guessing what was in store.

I swivelled away from the screen and looked out of the window again. The Baines Training Programme was well under way. Claire ran and Baines held the stop-watch. That was it as far as I could see. Probably exactly what she had in mind when she said he could help with the training. A time-keeper. Poor old Brains.

I watched her run a lap, very light and easy, her hair swishing from side to side. There were several people out there, but no other runners. Not even Metson. Maybe he'd given up training in shame. Most people were idling around in the sun, sitting in groups and taking no notice of Claire as she rounded the track on a great smooth curve. She passed Brains and he practically had a seizure with the watch, jumping about and waving his arms. I suppose he had to make it look good.

My name was still on the screen, sticking out from all the rest. As if it were calling attention to itself. "Hello, Gordon! It's me. Average age, average height. Nothing special." I didn't fancy the idea of looking at it any more so I switched on to another part of the program. Anything would've done, so long as I wasn't in it. As it happened, though, I called up the complete list of heights we'd fed into the computer on Friday. Hundreds of names and initials. I began to roll through till I got to myself again. Then I found I was moving the cursor along till it got to the height column, and adding three centimetres to the measurement against my name.

Brains: *A Summons*

Who should come looming into our Maths session that afternoon but Madge himself. A definite chill descended. He likes to think he has the measure of this place, but he never sees it the way it usually is. Every time he appears – which is not often – things change. Talk dries up. People find themselves fidgeting uncomfortably and they kind of shrink. Even Mr Peck kind of shrinks. Suddenly he is no longer gross but merely tubby and subdued. The rest of us feel we've got to be doing something and we set to work. If we can't handle the work we sit and look as if we're thinking deeply. This is not normal.

So Madge appeared in the doorway, hovering like a hawk and running his eyes over our faces. They settled on me.

"Ah," he breathed. "Trevor. Could you spare

Trevor for a moment or two, Mr Peck?"

And, of course, Peck could. I shouldn't think Madge Alsopp has heard anyone say no in years.

I stood up and felt as if I was leaving my blood behind. I was drained of will power and my mind began to list the crimes I'd committed over the past few days. There was nothing I'd done openly, but that didn't stop me worrying. Maybe he'd seen me in assembly the other morning and logged into my thoughts. I wouldn't put it past him. Things were going to be very sticky if he started questioning me about those. I'd been running this film in my head. Me and Mrs Posner, the science teacher, running naked through the corridors at night. Mrs Posner had given me a few cute smiles since the start of term so it seemed only natural to take things a little further. At least in my head.

We walked in silence to his room and he stood aside to let me in. I was convinced that Mrs Posner would be there, sitting at his desk with her legs crossed and staring accusingly at me. But the room was empty. He followed me in and shut off the outside world with a little push at the door.

"Now," he said, easing himself behind the desk. "Take a seat. I wanted a private word, Trevor. About a friend of yours."

"A friend?"

My voice squeaked. I sounded like an excited Brownie.

"Yes. Gordon Nesbitt. What can you tell me about him?"

Nesbitt! I'd never thought that name would

sound like music in my ears. What a relief it was to hear it. There were no problems with Nesbitt. I was in the clear.

"What did you want to know, sir?" I asked.

"Just what he's like. How you find him. I believe you're closer to him than the others. Am I right?"

"Well, he's ... erm ... er... He's all right..."

"All right?"

"Yes. I think so. Why?"

"I'm interested in his behaviour, Trevor. He's a quiet lad and I haven't quite fathomed him out yet. I like to get to know the people I'm supposed to educate..."

And on and on. Freud in a smart suit. I got the impression that he was disturbed by Noddy. He wanted to work him out, but there were pieces missing. I don't think I was much help.

"Has he any – what shall I say? – particular problems?" Alsopp continued.

"No," I said. "I don't think he's got any problems. Not specially. Just the usual things, you know."

He let me go. He wasn't interested in the usual things. He wanted to know about the unusual things. And there was nothing unusual about Nesbitt. Or if there was he'd have to find it himself.

Alsopp: *Memo to Self*

Trevor Baines no help. Just more time wasted. The only thing I achieved was to pass a message to Nesbitt via Baines. Shall see the lad myself. Keep it all rather casual. No special mention of the jacket débâcle. Then get on with running this school, which is what I'm paid to do.

Nesbitt: Some Interesting Facts About Averages

"The Average Pupil in the Average Week," said Ron Peck slowly. He was standing alone in the Humanities room and staring at a large sign propped against the board. Well, not quite alone. I was about to enter when I saw him and I stopped in the doorway.

"The Average Pupil in the Average Week," Peck repeated, even more slowly. "What the bloody hell is that supposed to mean?"

He screwed his plump face up, squinting at the letters to squeeze some meaning out of them, and jiggled his change in his trouser pocket. Peck was large. His belly, straining against the hammock of his shirt, rested precariously on his belt as if it might drop completely at any moment.

"Can I help, sir?" I asked, edging my way in.

"Ah, George. Explain this if you will. 'The Average Pupil in the Average Week.' What's she up to this time?"

"It's part of a Humanities project," I explained. (I didn't bother to tell him I wasn't George. Not worth the trouble.)

"I feared it might be," said Peck. "Hence our friend here, I suppose."

He nodded towards the dummy, which Miss

Cassidy had left at her desk. It had slid down since last I saw it and now looked as if it were sleeping off a binge.

"This is our Average Pupil, sir."

"Pity. I thought it might've been a new member of your form. I should've realized, I suppose. It looks too alert for one thing."

"No, sir. It's part of the project."

"Of course. Interesting, is it?"

"Sort of."

"And sort of a waste of time too."

"Why's that, sir?"

"Because there's no such thing as the Average Week. Especially round here. It doesn't exist."

The rest of the form straggled in and sat down. Peck eased his backside on to the edge of the desk and waited with folded arms. The usual triangle of crumpled shirt had escaped from his trousers.

"You'll be sorry to hear that Miss Cassidy is not with us this afternoon," he said. "She's on a course. A great shame for you, but the blow is considerably softened by the fact that I am standing in for her. Some of you may not realize how lucky you are to have me here."

"Does this mean we've got to do Maths instead, then?" moaned Dawn.

"Not necessarily, Dawn," he beamed. "My role is simply that of child-minder. Yours is that of toiler in the realms of Humanity, whatever that may mean, forging on with what you have already started. However, love of my subject forces me to point out a fundamental error in what you are doing. I was just telling George here that there is no such thing as an Average Week. Which renders your task tricky, to say the least."

"Why?" asked Brains. Just the question Peck was waiting for someone to ask. And Brains was just the person to ask it.

"Why is it tricky or why is there no Average Week?"

"Yes, sir."

"I see. Well, to take the last question first, there is no Average Week because each week is marked by events which make it different from all other weeks."

"Each seems pretty average to me," said Dawn.

"Seems, Dawn? Nay, I know not seems. Consider this week, for example. Would you say this week is average?"

"Yes. Very average."

"It can't be *very* average, can it? And this is certainly not an average week."

"Why not?"

"Because, for a start, Miss Cassidy isn't here and she usually is. Even if she were there'd be something else which set it apart. Some fluke of weather, say, or some peculiar behaviour on the part of one or more of you which made the week unusual."

"What about the Average Pupil?" I asked.

"Quite," said Peck with relish. "An even shakier concept. There can be no Average Pupil because, although you all look pretty average to a man of my intellect, the Average Pupil is an entirely mythical beast."

"A what?" asked Brains.

"Like our patient friend here," he said giving a

jerk of his head towards the slumped dummy. "It doesn't really exist."

"Why not?"

"Why not? Why not? Let me give you a f'rinstance." He rocked himself to his feet and began to pace. "I am a batsman of some class... Don't smirk, Baines... I go to the wicket and I score a dashing fifty. Exactly fifty. The next time I go to the wicket I score a brilliant fifty-one. Having a mathematical mind, I am curious to know what my average is. I do a little sum and work out that my average is ... what?"

"Fifty point five," said Dawn.

"Fifty point five. Yes. Or rather no. My average is the number of runs I have scored, evened out over all the innings I've played. But," he said, with a wave of his finger, "how can I possibly score fifty point five? I mean, what is point five of a run?"

"Half a run, sir?"

"Half a run indeed, Baines. And what happens in the next match when I score half a run?"

"Well, you get half way down the wicket..." I said.

"Exactly. And I am run out..."

"I don't get this," said Dawn.

"The point is, there is no such thing *in the real world* as half a run. Either a run *is* or it *isn't*. Half a run doesn't exist."

"Actually, I think cricket is the most boring game ever invented," said Dawn.

Brains frowned. "You mean, if you're the Average Pupil, you don't exist either?" he asked.

"Not strictly speaking. Anyone *might* be average

65

in some way but it wouldn't follow from that that he or she was *absolutely* average. He would certainly be *un*average in any number of other ways."

All that, if I could understand it properly, was something of a relief to me. One or two little things – the computer lists, the odd comment by Brains – had made me feel as if I was, well, ordinary. But I wasn't really. Not if Peck was right. No one could be ordinary. There was something about me that made me different from everyone else. All I had to do was find out what it was. I felt cheered.

The Really Last Meeting of the L.S.A.A.S. (Reformed)

All members present, but not for long. J. Corduroy proposed that we forget Athletics and become a fan club. F. Whale said who of? and J. Corduroy said she didn't know. There was a brief discussion about how you can have a fan club without someone to be fans of. S. James and F. Whale said they refused to become fans of any singer and suggested some rather flashy-looking actress. They even produced a much-thumbed photo. M. de Beere (Chair) said that, from the look of her, she didn't need any more fans. S. James then said he had to go early. J. Corduroy said we could be fans of Puerile Soaps and then S. James wouldn't have to keep sloping off. It was decided to look for a subject for the club. Until we decide who to support we are to be called The Fan Club Club.

(M. de B.)

Brains: *Nesbitt Hits the Limelight*

It was Claire who first noticed it. There was a lull in the room – the only sounds were the clatter of keys and Dawn mumbling complaints to herself under her breath – when Claire said to anyone who might be listening, "Nesbitt, G. I keep getting Nesbitt, G. Anyone know who that is?"

"Nesbitt?" I said. "You don't know little old Nesbitt? That's Nesbitt skulking in the corner."

"Oh," Claire said. "Him?"

The back of Noddy's neck started to go pink and he crouched closer to his screen, pretending he couldn't hear.

"What's he been up to, then?" I asked.

"He keeps cropping up on my lists. Look. Average age. Number of hours spent watching television. See, there he is again. Nesbitt, G. Weight. Nesbitt, G..."

The rest of the group started to gather round. It was like a scene from a film. The air traffic controller says, "I have an unidentified flying object on the radar," and all his colleagues come to look over his shoulder and it all goes quiet.

After a couple of minutes Noddy was the only one still working at his own screen. Except that he wasn't working – I could tell. He was jiggling at the keys and listening to every word.

"Noddy, come and look at this," I called. "This is amazing..."

"What is?" he asked and strolled over as casually as he could manage. Not too convincing.

"It looks as if we've found our Average Pupil,"

67

said Dawn. "I might've guessed it would be Nesbitt."

"There's no such thing as an Average Pupil," said Noddy loftily. "It's an idea without substance."

"Rubbish," said Dawn, her eyes still fixed on Claire's screen. "It's you. Look at this. You're in every list. The only one. We won't need Cassidy's stupid dummy now. We've got our own."

"That doesn't make me average. It's a coincidence..."

"He's right," said Claire. "He can't be *completely* average. Anyway, he's not on two of the lists."

"Which ones, which ones?" I asked.

"Siblings for one..."

"Whats?"

"Brothers and sisters. And there's no one on that list because the average number of children per family is two and a half..."

"And you can't have half a brother or half..." Noddy began, no doubt recalling Peck's words of wisdom about cricket. But midway through the sentence he dried up and I knew what he was thinking.

"Yes, you can!" I said. "He can, anyway. His sister is a what's-her-name, a half-sister! Isn't she, Nesbitt? Jeanette is your Mum's daughter from her first marriage, isn't she?"

"Why not open the door?" said Noddy. "Then you can shout it up and down the corridor."

Every face was suddenly focused on his. What was this odd specimen they were looking at?

"It's sort of creepy, isn't it?" said Dawn in a hushed voice. "I'm not sure I like it."

Up to now people had seen me moving about the place, here and there; sort of in the way, but not much more than that. Now they were looking at me as if they wanted to see inside me and read my thoughts. Dawn said it was sort of creepy and for a moment they just stood there looking at me in silence.

"Just a minute," I said. "There are two lists I'm not on. I can't be average if I'm not on the other list too, can I?"

But as soon as I said it I knew I should've kept my mouth shut. If only I'd laughed it off: "Average? Me? So I am. What a laugh." But no, I had to protest, and look nervous and guilty. And blush.

"What's the other list?" snapped Brains.

"Height," said Claire. "He's taller than average."

"Taller? Nesbitt?" said Dawn. "Are you sure?"

Claire tapped at the keyboard and another list appeared before their ravenous eyes.

"There you are," she said. "Average height. No Nesbitt. I checked and he's three centimetres taller."

"Double check!" said Dawn.

"Oh no..." I said. "Look, this has gone..."

But they just went mad. They bundled me against the wall, hands grabbing all over the place. I didn't stand a chance. Someone forced my head back and made a mark on the wall with a pencil. Dawn whipped out a tape measure. Typical of her to have a tape measure on her. She was like one of those knitters calling for blood at the foot of the guillotine. They shoved me aside to check the height of the mark.

And yes, they found exactly what they were looking for. Well, of course they did. Only three centimetres between me and the dummy, and I'd added them myself. The rest of the group huddled together, staring at me. This is great, I thought. It's only a matter of time before they start throwing bits of garlic at me and making the sign of the cross.

"Stone me," said Brains. "Bang on. It's weird."

"Utterly average," said Claire.

"Normal Nesbitt," added Dawn, peering at me with a look of distaste on her face.

Normal Nesbitt. That's what I was. I couldn't get the thought out of my head. It was still there long after I got home, and I felt the need to talk about it.

"What do you notice about me this evening?"

Colin lifted one eyebrow and looked up from his bowl on the kitchen floor. His tongue hung sideways out of his mouth as it often did when he was thinking.

"You're fed up?" he said.

"Simpler than that. What am I wearing?"

"What are you wearing?"

"On my feet?"

"Socks?"

"Socks. Yes. And what colour are they?"

"Grey."

"Good. Yes. And what about the trousers?"

"Grey as well."

"And the jumper?"

"Grey."

70

"I'm completely grey. From head to foot."

"So you are. Is that anything to get worked up about?"

"I'm not just talking about my clothes, Colin. I'm talking about me; the whole of me. Grey. Dull. Boring. Neither one thing nor the other. Halfway. Forgettable. The sort of person it's easy to ignore. Am I right?"

A vacant expression had settled across his doggy features and he made no reply.

"Colin?"

He wasn't even listening!

"Colin!"

"Sorry, sorry," he said. "Just my little joke."

"It's not a joking matter. Not any more."

"Go on, then. I am listening really. You're average, right?"

"Right. You remember what I was saying the other day about Holloway getting my name wrong?"

"Yes. He called you Niblett. And I said, never mind, you should be used to that because a lot of them get your name wrong."

"That's right; and some of them don't even know who I am in the first place. Madge tried to chuck me out because he thought I was from St Peter's, wherever the hell that is."

"Yes. I remember."

"Well, now I know why."

"Because you wear grey socks?"

"Because I'm average. Straight down the middle. There's nothing that sets me apart from any of the others so why should they know who I am?"

71

"I see," said Colin. "And what makes you think this? I mean, if there's any truth in it, why have you only just noticed it?"

"The computer program we've been running for Humanities. They're trying to come up with the Average Pupil. Peck says there's no such thing, but the computer says different. The computer says it's Nesbitt. Yours truly."

"And you think the computer is right?"

"I've been thinking about myself, Colin. I *am* average; I *am* dull. I'm not surprised people can't remember my name. I'm so dull I'm afraid I might forget it myself."

"I'll always remind you."

"Oh, thanks. Very sympathetic."

"Sorry, Gordon, but I must say I think you're taking it all too seriously. Does it matter if you're average? I might be an average dog – I've never thought about it before – but, even if I am, so what?"

"You might be quite happy to be an average dog, Colin, but I'm not happy to be an average pupil, or an average anything. I don't want to be the same, I want to be different. Not very different, just a little different will do, but still different."

Minutes of the First Official Meeting of the Fan Club Club

Three members present. Suggestions were put forward for subjects to be fans of. The voting was as follows: Ian Botham: 2 for, 1 against; Madonna:

2 for, 1 against; Kevin Costner: 1 for, 1 against, 1 abstention; Dennis the Menace: 3 against (M. de Beere pointed out that he's already got a fan club). The meeting was about to decide between Ian Botham and Madonna when the fourth member (J. Corduroy) turned up and said that her sister, Dawn, had told her of a bloke in her Humanities group who was completely average. She explained what this meant and there was heated debate about it until S. James proposed that we should adopt him for the club. At least we could keep an eye on him which wouldn't be so easy with the other two candidates. J. Corduroy said his name was Nisbett. We then voted unanimously to become the Average Nisbett Fan Club.

(M. de B.)

Brains: *Making Money Again*

I found Toby by the steps down to the boiler room. Some lower school kids were screeching about over a game of football and it wasn't easy to conduct a business deal.

"No," Toby said. "I'm not taking any bets till I've seen a full list of runners."

"But you know she'll be in it so why can't you just take one little bet on her?"

"A tenner isn't a little bet, Baines."

A couple of mad first years, knees and elbows all over the place, bundled headlong towards us after a dented football. I stepped aside as they cannoned into the railings of the boiler room steps and bounced off again. I watched them go, lowered my voice and edged closer to Toby.

"Listen, I'm taking a big risk here. I'm not saying she'll be in the first ten. I'm not even saying she'll be in the first three. I'm saying she'll win. Now, why can't you take my money?"

"Because the betting's not open yet. Once I know the runners I'll work out the odds and I'll be happy to take your tenner off you. I know what you're up to. You want to get your bet in before word gets round and the odds shorten."

The bell sounded and brought the meeting to a close. For the time being. I'd have to work on Toby again later. As we went into school Nesbitt joined us. He was looking grey in the face and as miserable as sin.

"I'm not risking a tenner unless the odds are good," I said.

"This is the Halliwell Bowl, I take it," said Noddy without much enthusiasm.

"I don't see why he can't start his book now. The list's been up for ages and this is the last day for entering. Anyone who's going to put in for it has already signed up..."

"I don't know," I heard him say. "I haven't put in for it yet."

"You, Nesbitt?" I asked. Was I hearing properly?

"Why not?"

Why not? There were plenty of reasons why not. For a start it wasn't his style. I just couldn't see him standing up to the strain of press-ups night and day, or exposing his pink legs to the public. In fact, I couldn't think of any reasons why he *should* go in for it. None that made sense. I think he only said it on the spur of the moment. Maybe because he was miffed about what the computers had churned out about him.

"It's a race, Gordon, a proper race. For runners, not plodders."

"I'm entitled to enter, aren't I? It's an open race."

"If you're trying to get in on my training sessions," I said, "you can forget it. She's running by herself till the race."

"She can train in a vacuum for all I care," he said. "I just thought I'd enter, that's all."

"Well, I don't get it. You're up to something, Gordon, but I can't work out what it is."

Nesbitt: Plans and Motives

Brains was right – I was up to something. It was simple enough, really. Only I wasn't telling him. Not yet, anyway. I did tell Colin. I had to explain it to someone, just so that I could be sure I wasn't being completely barmy. Besides, Colin needed to know, because it was going to change the pattern of our evening walks.

"You see, if I put my guts into it, I could do quite well," I told him.

We were on our way to the park and he wasn't terribly keen to be out.

"Do we have to?" he whined, sounding just like Stuart.

"Yes, we do. This is going to be a training session, Colin, not simply a walk."

"So you think you can win? Beat Metson and the Dumb Blonde?"

"No. That's not the point. I don't have to win. All I have to do is finish in the top half. Anywhere, as long as it isn't halfway. I've got to prove that I'm not average."

We went in through the park gates and I broke into a run. Colin loped along at my heels.

"But why me?" he snapped. Not like him to be snappy. "I'm not running in the Halliwell blinking Bowl, am I?"

"Don't moan. This is going to be good for both of us."

We jogged along in silence for several minutes. I thought he was sulking, but, in fact, he was mulling things over.

"There's an easier way than this," he panted eventually.

"Oh, yes?"

"Yes. You could come last."

"What?"

"Don't try too hard. Let yourself come last, or finish well down the field..."

"What's the point of that?"

"Well, if you're last you're not average, are you?"

I thought about this while we ran the length of the boating lake and into the little wood where we first saw Claire.

"That wouldn't work," I said. "It would be cheating. I mean, I'd *know* I was coming last on purpose. It's too easy."

Colin slowed down and began to drag on the lead.

"Do you mind if we stop and rest?" he said. "I'm no greyhound, you know."

"OK. You stay here. I'll go once more round the lake."

When I got back to him he'd found a patch of late sun filtering through the trees and looked as if he were asleep.

"Come on," I said. "Let's go home."

"Walking?"

"Yes, walking."

"I thought of something else while you were struggling round the lake..."

"I wasn't struggling, Colin, I can assure you of that. I feel pretty good as a matter of fact. I should've been doing this ages ago."

"Hmm." He didn't sound convinced. "If this is an open race and it's mostly the athletic types who go in for it, how is that going to prove that you're better than average?"

"Say that again."

"I mean they're all going to be more or less good, aren't they? The no-hopers aren't even going to enter. Apart from you."

"I'm not a no-hoper. I'm very determined."

"But you're not one of the favourites either. I mean, you said yourself, you haven't got a torso like Metson, have you?"

"I suppose not."

"And your aim is to finish where?"

"Somewhere in the top half, Colin. That'll do me."

"Right. So it's not going to be that easy, is it? A really average person like you is going to finish in the *bottom* half of a field of good runners. Am I right?"

"I don't know. Are you?"

"So, to finish in the top half you've really got to pull all the stops out, haven't you?"

"I suppose so," I said. I hadn't thought of it like that before.

"Well, Gordon," said Colin, "I have to say I don't think you're going to make it."

Alsopp: *Memo to Self*

Called Gordon Nesbitt in for a chat. At last. Asked the usual questions. How are you settling in? What plans do you have for the future? Any problems? I do this quite often, and although I give the impression that it's all very informal and pleasant, I'm working hard at stocking up the memory banks. Not easy in this case. The lad is quite forgettable. All he seemed to say was "all right", "not too bad" and "yes, thank you". He wasn't building up a solid picture at all. The only twitch of interest came with the any problems question. He hesitated. I asked again and he muttered something about not being good at anything.

"That doesn't mean you're bad at things, though, does it, Gordon?" I suggested.

"Oh, no," he said. "I'm not bad either."

A strange thing, but I got the impression that he wished he *was* bad at something. I detect a psychological imbalance somewhere. I had to cut the meeting short in order to dash off to Shire Hall with the usual begging bowl, but, I regret to say, I feel I should follow this one up. Nesbitt looks and sounds fairly normal but sometimes they're the ones who need watching.

Minutes of the First Meeting of the Average Nisbett Fan Club

All present. The first item on the agenda was the name of the Club. J. Corduroy now says that our celebrity is called Nesbitt, not Nisbett. In fact her sister says that he is known as Normal Nesbitt. Unanimously accepted that we change our name to The Normal Nesbitt Fan Club. F. Whale said we had more names for the club than we had members, but I think this one will stick. The next thing we decided was to go out and do some Nesbitt-spotting. Results to be pasted into a scrapbook. Quite a bit of enthusiasm for this. It's something to do for a change, rather than just sitting around and talking.

(M. de B.)

Brains: *The Strain Begins to Show*

He wasn't happy. You didn't have to be Freud to see that. He was stalking up the corridor, looking as if he could punch holes in the wall.

"What's up?" I asked. "Why the mood?"

He didn't answer. We swept round a corner and came across Miranda de Beere, Jo Corduroy and a couple of others. They were gathered in a tight circle, sniggering over something. This is the usual way with second year girls. They'd snigger at a funeral if they got the chance. One of them looked up as we approached and hissed, "Look out! It's him."

Nesbitt forged straight through them, scattering them like geese. They flapped and squealed, and as they scuttled off Miranda dropped the something they'd been sniggering about. I stooped to pick it up.

"Hey," I said. "This is you."

He turned round to face me, breathing hard through his nostrils. What I had in my hand was a ragged copy of the school newspaper. The school paper came out once every half term, more or less. It usually had a few pages of sports round-ups, the odd poem nobody understood, some jokes about the staff and a letter of complaint from Dawn. That kind of stuff. Usually no one takes much notice, but this time it had something that caught the attention. On the front page was a badly produced photograph. Of Nesbitt. With his mouth hanging open. "Is this Mr Average?" said the caption, and beneath was an article spelling it all out.

"Noddy," I said. "You've made the papers. Front page."

"So I have. Isn't that wonderful?"

"Aren't you pleased? I would be."

"Do I look pleased?"

He didn't. I could tell. Partly by the way he narrowed his eyes at me and partly because he snatched the paper and ripped it in half, slapping the pieces back into my hand.

"But what's wrong with it?" I asked, a bit taken aback by this un-Nesbitt-like display. "It's only a bit of fun, isn't it?"

"Oh, sure. A bit of fun for everyone else."

"It doesn't mean anything..."

"Of course it does," he said, marching off. "It means I'm a pillock. A laughing stock."

"Yes, but..."

"And I don't like it!"

We reached the dining hall and he kicked open the door. Immediately the buzz of chatter died and everyone looked up. For about two seconds there was absolute silence. Out of the corner of my eye I saw Dawn gawping at us, or, to be more precise, at Nesbitt, with her lips still pursed against a glass of water. Then the chatter broke out again. Only more so. It's him. Mr Average. Normal Nesbitt. Snigger snigger. I glanced at Noddy and thought he was looking dangerous. Dangerous for him, anyway.

"Look, Gordon," I said. "Don't do anything silly..."

"Silly, Brains? How can I do anything silly? Silly people do silly things. I'm not a silly person. I'm an average person. Don't you read the papers?"

Before I could try a little calming influence, he was off again. He'd noticed Jackie sitting in a corner and was making straight for her.

"Well, well, well, if it isn't our little photographer friend," he said, towering over her.

Or rather not towering. Looking down from a normal sort of height. Average people *don't* tower, do they? And this was what was bugging him.

Nesbitt: Doing Something Positive at Last

They can't do things like that, I thought. They can't get away with it. (Well, they could get away with it if I let them. The way I let them get away with calling me by the wrong name or trying to chuck me out of school. So this time I wasn't going to sit back and let it happen.) I went straight to the source of the trouble. Jackie Maugham.

She could see that something was up.

"Oh, hello," she said, a sort of innocent simper on her face.

I don't know how she managed it. To look innocent, I mean. A *photographer*; the lowest of the low. The sort of gutter scum who snoop about looking for people in trouble and, instead of offering a helping hand, *take pictures*.The sort of rats who creep through bushes on their bellies and take shots of the Royal Family picking its nose.

"Hi, Jackie," said Brains in a pathetic attempt to smooth things over. "How's tricks?"

"I'll tell you how tricks are," I snarled. "Tricks are rather dirty at the moment."

"Oh," said Jackie. "You've seen the paper?"

"What makes you think that?" I asked with a bitter laugh.

"Look, Gordon, it was only a picture..."

"Oh, yes. Only a picture. Only a picture that happens to make every little pip-squeak first and second year laugh its head off whenever it sees me."

"I didn't mean..."

82

"And don't tell me you didn't mean it, because you should've *thought* first."

"They needed a shot of you, that's all."

"Why didn't you ask? It's my face."

"Of course it's your face, but your face is public property, Gordon."

"Bollocks."

"No, just your face."

She was being unreasonably composed under the onslaught of my anger. I thought she might've cowered a bit, at least.

"You might think it's yours," she explained, "and, in a way, it is because it's stuck to you, but you don't have to look at it, do you?"

"What's that supposed to mean?"

"You only see it in a mirror. The rest of us see it whenever you're about. In that sense it belongs to us all."

"She's got a point there, Noddy," said Brains.

"Shut up, Brains."

I sat down and thought hard. What I wanted was a row, not a debate.

"Anyway," Jackie went on, "it was just a picture. What's got your knickers in a twist is the article that went with it."

Yes. Precisely. That was the point. Condemned out of her own mouth. I tapped the table with my knuckles.

"Precisely," I said. "Cheap, gutter journalism with no thought for those it damages. What about that?"

"That may be," she said, "but I didn't write the article."

She didn't? I wasn't expecting that. No wonder she was looking so calm.

"Then who did?" I said, glaring suddenly at Brains.

"Don't look at me," he said. "I didn't write it. I didn't even see it till just now. And anyway I'm a lousy writer, Noddy, you know that."

"Then who...?"

Brains: *Will You Ever Be Able to Trust Women?*

I always said blondes were the cruel ones. I mean, what was she thinking about, doing a thing like that to poor old innocent Gordon Nesbitt? It didn't seem fair. What made it worse, of course, was that he had this crush on her. Of all the girls shimmying about the place he had to pick on her. Why?

Well, I knew why, really. Blonde hair. A lovely face. Graceful movement. And, not to put too fine a point on it, those neat, neat breasts. No need to put too fine a point on those. With women, you see, you have to be very clear in your mind. You have to separate the two key aspects of women. Their minds and their bodies. If you think a tasty body means a generous mind you can find yourself very quickly in a nasty place without a paddle. You have to know what you're dealing with. Get it clear. On the one hand she's capable of being a right bitch. On the other she looks bloody fantastic. Fine. If you know that, you know where you stand. After all, you can't blame her breasts for the way she behaves, can you?

What makes it all so complicated is that you can see their bodies but you can't see their minds. Maybe if it were the other way round you could rid the world of lust altogether. Maybe the world would be a better place for it.

And maybe not.

Alsopp: *Memo to Self*

Nesbitt. I've opened a file on him. Of course, all my charges are on file, but this is a separate file, for my eyes only, at the moment. So far there is little in it: my observations on our first meeting – or rather, second meeting (I haven't mentioned the jacket incident); facts and figures from his records. These make extraordinary reading. He seems to be average in every subject. All his test scores indicate average ability, average intelligence, average achievement. Most of the comments from previous teachers tend to say the same thing. Average. Extraordinarily ordinary, you might say.

Caught sight of him in the corridor yesterday and was pleased with myself for recognizing him this time. Said hello, but he ploughed by without answering. In fact he was looking pretty grim. I assume he just didn't hear me. A little disturbing to think he might've heard and decided to ignore my friendly overture.

Nesbitt: The Consequences of Cruelty

When I knew that Claire had written the article in the school paper I felt pretty low about it. I was all steamed up to tell Jackie exactly what I thought of her and I found I was talking to the wrong person. I felt like a kettle boiling its guts out in an empty room.

"Are you going to face her with it?" Brains asked me.

"I've got a good mind to," I said.

But I didn't have a good mind to. I didn't have any mind to at all.

"I wouldn't advise it," said Brains.

"And why not?"

"Well, it could upset her training programme."

Thank you very much. She can say what she likes about me but I mustn't answer back in case it puts her off her running. Well, as long as we know where we stand.

In any case, what could I say to her? It was easy enough to shout at Jackie. I *knew* Jackie. But Claire I didn't know. I could just imagine her frosty look if I even so much as asked her about the article. So, I thought, let her stew. Let it rest on her conscience.

The years will pass and she'll go off and be beautiful and successful and win races all over the place and all the time, somewhere inside her, will be this niggling thought. "Through my cruel act I made this boy miserable," she'll think at the age of fifty or something, looking back over her life. "For the sake of a cheap joke. I wonder what became of him. I wonder where he is now. Is he wandering the

86

streets looking in waste-bins and sleeping on
benches? What was his name? Niblitt or something. Yes, that was it. Normal Niblitt."

I bet she won't even get my bloody name right.

Minutes of the First Meeting of the
Normal Nesbitt Fan Club

Off to a good start. The first item was pasted into
the Club Scrapbook. An article in the school paper
all about Gordon Nesbitt himself, complete with
picture. This has caused a lot of interest and two
new members have come forward to join us (K.
Hart and R. McCord).

The Nesbitt-spotting activity was less successful.
F. Whale and S. James failed to complete any
sightings at all. The photo in the paper should help
in future, though. On the plus side, the Club Chair
managed to extract from one of the simpler members of the Upper School (Brains) a copy of the
Nesbitt timetable, so it should be possible to know
his whereabouts at any point during any day. Some
discussion about whether Nesbitt-spotting should
take place after school hours. J. Corduroy reports
that N.N. has entered the Halliwell Bowl. Proposed
(by M. de B.) that a fan letter should be addressed
to Nesbitt. Individual members to work on this.

(M. de B.)

Well, I had to do something. I couldn't bring myself to challenge the Dumb Blonde, but I wanted to make some kind of positive gesture. I just couldn't think what. The only thing that occurred to me was to withdraw from the Halliwell Bowl. Which, really, was a negative thing, I suppose. A nothing reaction.

If anyone asked, I'd tell them I was pulling out because the whole business seemed rather petty to me.

"I'm sorry," I'd say, "but I think it's all too pointless. It's only a race and life isn't about races."

The trouble was that Brains was the only one who was likely to ask. And anyway I knew that the real reason was that I was simply fed up. Fed up to the back teeth, as Dad was fond of saying. I'd also been thinking about what Colin had said: that I'd have to be a better than average runner to finish even halfway. I was inclined to agree with him. I didn't have it in me.

So I went to seek out the Hunk and tell him.

He was in the P.E. store, heaving equipment around in one of his periodic tidy-ups.

"Ah," he said. "Friend Nesbitt. What can I do for you?"

It didn't escape my notice that he got my name right. I think I'd have felt better if he'd got it wrong.

"It's about the Halliwell Bowl," I said.

"Yes, of course. Well, I'm glad you've come, because I wanted a word with you about that."

"The thing is..." I began.

"It is, as you know, an open race," he cut in. "Anyone can run in it. It's also a district race. Half a dozen other schools will be taking part."

He lugged a huge roll of P.E. mat against a wall and sat down on it. A film of healthy sweat was shining on his face. There was something about his manner – perhaps something in his voice or the way he rested his elbows on his knees and looked up at me – that was different. Not the usual bustling, loud Holloway; the joky sergeant-major, respected by the lads and a scourge to all weeds.

"Don't get me wrong, Gordon," he said. "I'm glad you put your name down. It shows a bit more backbone than I thought you had. But I was wondering how much thought you'd put into it."

"I've thought a lot about it, sir," I said. "That's why I wanted to see you."

"So it wasn't a joke?"

"A joke? No, sir, but I wanted to ask—"

"Well, I think you need to consider it more carefully."

He was ploughing on with his speech, which, I guessed, he'd had worked out for some time. Probably something to do with extra training and working on technique and tactics. The Holloway Method of Health and Fitness. How to win races and influence people. I could've saved him the bother except that I couldn't really get a word in.

"As there will be so many runners from all over the place, and quite a lot of attention paid to it, we really want to turn out a smart squad. Especially as we're the hosts this year. I know it's open to volunteers, but it's not a soft option, you know. It's quite a gruelling race. We've got the runners to make a good showing. A pretty dedicated bunch. And Metson and the new girl will probably run well. To be honest, we've got a good chance of taking the team trophy. And that's the problem, really."

"Problem, sir?"

"Yes. I'd like you to drop out."

"Pardon?"

"If you come straggling in at the end of the field it could damage our chances. I don't like to discourage a lad who wants to compete, but you'd do best by the school if you didn't take part."

"I see."

Here I was, trying to tell him I wouldn't be running, and here he was, begging me to withdraw.

He stood up and started shifting pieces of equipment around again. He may even have been a little embarrassed.

"Think about it, will you, Gordon?" he said. "Come and see me at the end of the afternoon and tell me what you decide. OK?"

"OK, sir."

I went back outside and thought about it, like he said. But not for long. If Holloway wanted me to pull out because I wasn't up to it and because it would be the best thing for the school, for Queen and country and Claire Brooks, I decided that the best thing to do was to stay in. From that moment on I was determined to run in the Halliwell Bowl. And sod everyone else.

Brains: *Fame and Gordon Nesbitt*

He wasn't the same old Nesbitt any more. I'd seen him through a lot, showed him more ropes than he knew what to do with, and now he seemed to lose interest. I know he was feeling sick about the way things had gone with Claire, but that wasn't my fault, was it? If he'd listened to me in the first place things might've been very different.

But I'm not a hard-hearted man. I knew he was working things out. There comes a time in the life of every bloke when he suddenly finds himself face to face with himself. He looks in a mirror and he says, "Who is this? Just who the bloody hell is this looking out at me?" He has to face his Waterloo, or his Clacton or whatever. Before he faces it he doesn't know where he's going. Afterwards ... well, without knowing what's happened to him, he can handle himself. Every dilemma comes to him the same and he can cope. No sweat.

This has happened to me. I've been there before. A girl with a fringe of dark hair and clear blue eyes, the noise of a dance floor. You step outside, into the heart of Clacton at night, and ... well, you're not a kid any more. It's as simple as that.

I'm not talking about something physical, by the way. All that is much more mundane. This is more to do with that unmistakable but hard-to-define look in a man's eyes. You see it in Humphrey Bogart when he takes a fag out of his mouth. A certain look.

Anyway, I knew I had to let Gordon find his own particular Clacton.

91

What puzzled me, though, was the way he suddenly became popular. Everyone knew Nesbitt. Everyone was interested in Nesbitt. Miranda de Beere even bought his timetable off me. Nesbitt was the flavour of the month. Girls looked at him out of the corner of their eyes. Wondering what he was like. I mean, if he wasn't so moody about things, he could've spread himself about a bit, like butter on warm bread. He just didn't see it, though. And he wouldn't listen to me.

So, why were they all panting after Nesbitt all of a sudden? Because he was so ordinary. Mr Average. Weird. It's not an approach I'd've thought of, I must say.

Nesbitt: **A Kind of Sickness**

Colin and I walked by the river in silence. It wasn't that there was nothing to talk about. Far from it. I was anxious to get his views on Holloway's little speech about me being too useless – or too average I suppose I should say – to take part in the big race. The reason for the silence was that Jeanette had decided to come with us. You can't have a proper conversation with your dog if your sister is in tow.

She doesn't usually come out with us. Walking with Colin is too leisurely for Jeanette. In fact it isn't often that she walks anywhere. She's more inclined to dash. Dash off to the skating rink. Dash off to rehearsals for the latest play. In spite of all that dashing, though, she's hardly ever on time for things.

We walked along and nobody spoke. Well, Colin and I walked. Even when she had to cut down her pace so that she could stay level with us, Jeanette still didn't exactly walk. It was more a sort of bounce. She lobbed a few sticks for Colin and he wandered off to bring them back, but really it would've made more sense if he'd thrown the sticks for her.

At first I wondered why she'd bothered to come at all. I assumed it was to try out her new look. (She changes her look two or three times a month, sometimes so wildly that I don't recognize her. It's like living in a dressing room at the National Theatre with weird-looking people wandering in and out from some bizarre drama.) This latest one was all cropped hair and white skin with black eye make-up and lipstick. At a distance her face looked like an electric socket. But it wasn't her new look that had brought her out.

"Are you sick or something, Gordon?" she asked me.

"What?"

"Are you sick? You're acting peculiar these days. Mum thought you might have something wrong with you."

"Mum did?"

"Yes. Bowel movements or something. She asked me to make a few subtle enquiries."

It wasn't what I'd call subtle, coming straight out with it like that. (Look, Gordon, if you're seriously ill or something I wish you'd say so quickly because I've got things to do, places to be and I don't want to be held up by people who are sick.)

"Do I look sick?" I said.

"Not to me, no."

"Well, I'm not."

"That's all right, then," she said and bounced off, her duty done.

"Do I look sick?" I asked Colin when she'd gone.

"Not sick exactly."

"What then?"

"Miserable."

"Oh, thanks."

"Aren't you, then?"

"Miserable? Yes, I am, as a matter of fact."

"So you shouldn't be surprised if you look it, should you?"

"Yes, but she said 'peculiar'."

"Ah," said Colin. "If I were you I'd be quite pleased about that."

"Why?"

"Because peculiar isn't average, is it? And being average is what's getting you down. Am I right?"

"Among other things, yes."

I explained about the article in the school paper and Holloway asking me to withdraw from the race.

"Awful," said Colin.

"You really think so? You're not having me on?"

"I really think so. You have every right to enter that race. If I were you I'd go ahead no matter where I came. It's a principle."

"But it does matter where I come, Colin. I still want to prove I'm not average."

"Ah."

"What do you mean 'ah'?"

"That's not so easy, is it? You'll have to work at that one, I think, Gordon."

Colin wasn't always as comforting as he should've been. He didn't hold with the Man's Best Friend school of dog–master relationships. If he thought a thing was wrong he saw it as his duty to say so.

"You'd better get running," he said. "Down to the last boat house and back. I'll wait here and watch."

"Watch? What good will that do?"

"I'll observe your style. That'll be useful. And it'll save my legs."

So I glanced at my watch and set off along the river bank and under the bridge to the boat houses. But my mind wasn't on running. I kept thinking about Holloway and the Dumb Blonde; how, in their different ways, they were treating me like a jerk. So what if I was no one special? Was that a reason to exclude me from open races or to take the piss in public? The more I thought about it, pounding along between the river and the common, the angrier I became. The thump of my feet on the path became a thump of rage in my head.

By the time I got back to Colin my breath was rasping in my throat and there was a fierce heat inside me.

"Well, well," said Colin, his brow wrinkled in surprise. "I may have to change my opinion about this."

"Why?" I gasped.

"Because that looked fast to me, Gordon. Faster than you've ever been before."

I was slightly surprised by this because, as I say, I wasn't thinking about the running. However, I looked at my watch and my watch confirmed it. A personal best. Which was a valuable lesson to me. It isn't just legs and lungs that get you going; it's an anger inside.

Minutes of the Second Meeting of the Normal Nesbitt Fan Club

Eight members present. More items were added to the scrapbook. A letter to Normal Nesbitt was put together and read out.

Dear Mr Nesbitt,

We are keen supporters of you and admirers of your style. We would like you to know that we are following your career with great interest. It's good to hear that you will be running in the Halliwell Bowl and you can be sure that we will all be there to cheer you on. Would you be kind enough to answer some questions for us? Where were you born and on what day? What are the names of members of your family? What are your hobbies? We feel sure that your interests will be ours too. If you could send us your autograph and any other personal items for our collection we would be extremely grateful.

Yours sincerely,
The Normal Nesbitt Fan Club

Sightings of N.N. have increased greatly since our

last meeting. S. James pointed out that some interesting changes to the appearance of our celebrity were taking place and F. Whale suggested that we should take careful note of these. It was agreed to run a Normal Nesbitt competition, open to club members only. There was some discussion about what form this competition should take, but so far no one has thought of anything decent. J. Corduroy suggested making Normal Nesbitt bookmarks, but this was defeated on a vote. We really want something more active.

(M. de B.)

Brains: *Coming to Terms With Nesbitt's Hair*

When he turned up looking – well, looking the way he did – I thought, what have we got here? What sort of state must his mind be in, I asked myself, to do that to his hair?

He'd put globules of gel on his head and raked his fingers through it to make it stand up. It looked as if some kind of limp sea anemone had fixed itself on top of his head. The anemone seemed to be moving of its own will, as if it was looking for food. I didn't know whether to mention this or not. On the one hand I didn't like to draw attention to the fact that he was looking a proper plonker. On the other hand it was hard not to say something.

We were in the woodwork huts, working away at our ever-shrinking lamps. We'd been working on these lamps for as long as I could remember. They'd started out as proper-sized table lamps, but

97

by now they were dwindling into toothpicks. I let some time slip by, casually, as if nothing was wrong. Then I dropped a careful hint.

"Where did you get the gel from?" I asked.

"Gel?" he said vaguely.

"Have you put gel on your hair, Noddy, or have you just walked under a pigeon with diarrhoea?"

He wouldn't say, but I guessed he'd got it from Jeanette, his sister. Jeanette was an expert in changing her appearance. One day she could look like Dracula's cleaning lady and the next an electrocuted parrot. It depended on her mood. (Actually, the Dracula look could be quite stirring. If I wasn't so strict with myself about older women...)

Anyway, it was really obvious what poor old Nesbitt was up to – trying to change himself. He thought that all you had to do was change your appearance and your personality would follow suit. That might work with someone like Jeanette, but Noddy was out of a different mould.

Well, as usual he'd made a complete botch of it so I thought the kindest thing was to change the subject.

"So, you're really going to run?" I asked.

"Yes. I don't see why I shouldn't."

"No, no. Of course not. What did Hunk say when you told him?"

"He didn't like it much," Noddy said. "Scowled a bit and went red in the face. Then he said it was up to me."

"Fine. Great. Why not?"

"That's what I thought."

"So maybe you'd like to join the training sessions."

"What?"

I could see the bolting bunny look come over his face.

"After all," I added, "if you're running in the Halliwell Bowl, Noddy, you've got to practise, haven't you?"

"I thought you said you didn't want me along."

"I don't mind," I said. "In fact, it might make things a bit more interesting if you came out as well. I don't think Claire will object."

He said nothing about that. Instead he took his lamp off the bench and frowned at it.

"Which way up was this supposed to be? Can you remember?" he asked.

"The wide bit goes at the bottom."

"There isn't a wide bit. It's the same all the way down. I think I'm going to have to take a bit off one end," he said. "So I can tell the difference."

Dan, the woodwork man, sauntered up behind him and looked over his shoulder. He thought about saying something, I could tell, but he changed his mind and moved on. It was pretty clear that Nesbitt had reached the point where advice was a waste of time. I knew how Dan felt.

"Has Toby worked out the odds yet?" Noddy asked.

"Don't talk to me about that shyster. He's got Claire at three to one for a place in the first five. And he won't accept a tenner, either."

"Why not?"

"Because he knows she'll do it, that's why. If

only he'd taken my bet when I first mentioned it. I could've made a small fortune, Noddy. A small fortune."

He picked up a chisel and started digging violently at one end of his lamp.

"What's the betting on the rest of the field?"

"Metson's five to one which he doesn't like very much. Being second favourite. You can get good odds on some of the others, but it's not worth the risk, in my opinion."

"What about the team trophy?"

"Dead stingy. Four to one. It was even worse – two to one – but when you said you were still in it the odds lengthened a bit."

"Great," he said. "Nice to know people have confidence in you."

"Actually, there's quite a lot of money on you, according to Toby. You can get a fair bet on..."

He stopped hacking away at his lump of wood and gave me a curious look. Time to change the subject again, I thought.

"This lamp. I'm not sure I'm doing the right thing. Maybe I should go and have a word with Dan."

"Just a minute," he said. "You can get a fair bet on what?"

"Well, you know Toby. He'll bet on anything."

"Brains. What's the bet?"

Well, he insisted on knowing so what could I do? I told him.

"That you'll finish in the middle of the field," I said. "Anywhere in the middle ten."

"Oh, wonderful."

"Don't take it so seriously. It's only a game..."

"A game? I thought you said there was a lot of money on me."

"There is, but, well, it's just a laugh, isn't it? Nothing to get worked up about."

"I'm not getting worked up about it," he said with a sniff. "It's no skin off my nose."

Nesbitt: The New Look

But, of course, I *was* getting worked up about it. Inside. I just wasn't going to let Brains know.

So, it was fixed in everyone's mind that I was Mr Average. A couple of weeks ago hardly anyone knew who I was. Now my name was on all lips. And my right name too. Nesbitt. Or, as everyone now called me, Normal Nesbitt. I had a real piss-taking letter from a Normal Nesbitt Fan Club, which I screwed into a tiny ball and flushed down the loo where it belonged. It was almost certainly from the Dumb Blonde, who was probably laughing up her sleeve at all this.

And Brains expected me to join his training sessions with her. Claire wouldn't mind, he said. I wasn't so sure about that. I could just hear her saying, "Normal Niblett? I don't want *him* getting under my feet. Tell him to go away." And I'd have to slink off, pretending I didn't mind. Besides, I didn't want to train at school. All my running was done in the evenings down by the river, when no one was about. It suited me to let Brains, or anyone else for that matter, think that I wasn't doing any training at all. Let them think I was a no-hoper.

And then let them watch me run.

I was disappointed that no one seemed to pay much attention to my new look. I'd taken quite a bit of trouble over it. People should've noticed, because up till then my hair had always been the same – shortish, tidyish with a sort of parting in more or less the usual place. In fact it felt as if I'd been born with it. Popped out to meet the world with a decent hair-cut and a proper parting. Time to try something different, I thought.

So I lingered in the bathroom one morning and smeared a handful of Jeanette's gel on my head. I tried moving the parting – left, right, further right, in the middle. It didn't seem to make much difference. The centre-parting made me look like a Victorian undertaker, which wasn't what I was after, but otherwise I remained the same old, dull, horribly normal Gordon Nesbitt.

Mum didn't recoil with shock when she saw it, as I thought she might. She carried on pottering about until she put the usual bowl of cereal in front of me. Then she stopped and squinted at me, looking worried and running her hand over my forehead.

"Are you all right, Gordon?" she said. "Did Jeanette have a word with you?"

"Yes, she did. And I'm perfectly all right, thank you."

"I don't know. You look a little bit ... greasy to me. You're not constipated, are you?"

Constipation is Mum's big worry. It worries her far more than nuclear power or the ozone layer. If they had a protest movement about it, with badges and marches, she'd be right in the forefront with her banner: HAVE YOU BEEN TO THE TOILET TODAY? According to her, constipation is responsible for almost everything that's wrong with society, from graffiti to football hooligans. I think she'd like it taught properly in schools, with a chance to take a GCSE in it.

I promised her that I wasn't constipated and she seemed satisfied. She said nothing about the hair.

The only one who made any fuss at all was Jeanette, who had a screaming fit at me that night for stealing her gel. I tried to tell her Stuart had pinched it to make a skid-pad for his vehicles but she wasn't having any of it.

I made several other attempts to change my lifestyle when the gel failed. I took to wearing different coloured socks, for example. One green and one blue. The sort of thing normal people just don't do; a little touch to make me stand out from the crowd. But it didn't work. After a day or two, several of the younger kids started turning up in odd socks. I could hardly believe it to begin with. First one kid in odd socks, then another, and another. And most of them had gel daubed all over their heads as well. It gave me a weird feeling in the base of my spine.

Odd socks is now the norm, I thought. Maybe I've created a fashion. Either that or I'm following a fashion without even realizing I'm doing it. Which is worse.

Minutes of the Third Meeting of the Normal Nesbitt Fan Club

Ten members present. There has been no response to our fan letter. This is disappointing but not disastrous. Nesbitt remains a mystery to us, admired from afar. Several members have been following N.N.'s lead in looks by smothering their hair in gel and wearing different coloured socks. F. Whale said it was a shame that some non-members were attempting the same kind of thing, but there's not much we can do about that. Except, of course, persuade them to join us. Obviously they're following Normal Nesbitt too, but in an unofficial kind of way.

Competition news! It has been decided that the first Nesbitt competition will be a test of observation skills. The member who observes and notes down the largest number of new facts about our celebrity will win. Everyone to contribute twenty pence towards a prize. S. James (who, by the way, has missed the last two weeks of his Puerile Soap) said how would we know if the things observed were real or made-up. M. de Beere suggested that each observation should be backed up by evidence – a photo or the signature of a third party or something.

(M. de B.)

Alsopp: *Memo to Self*

Each meeting with Nesbitt only made me think I should see him again. Couldn't work the boy out. Sometimes thought he was merely an innocent fool and sometimes concluded he had the brain of a master criminal. Most of the time, wish I could forget him and return to the full-time business of running the school. The file I've started on him gets larger and larger. In fact it's three files now and takes up a complete shelf in the corner of my room.

However, think I've cracked it. Have made a few more enquiries. Had a word with Holloway and Miss Cassidy. Also called in some of his work and studied it. The work was very revealing and by the time I'd finished going through it I thought I could see a way ahead. The boy is clearly disturbed and I have devised a strategy for him to face up to this disturbance in himself. Have sent for him again, but the meeting will need very careful handling. Very careful indeed.

Nesbitt: **More Meetings With Madge**

Things have changed since Alsopp nearly frog-marched me off the premises because of the jacket. The last time I saw him he had an oily smile ready and a cup of tea with a thin biscuit balanced in the saucer.

"I've been looking at your work, Gordon," he said. "It's interesting. Very interesting."

That was encouraging. I've never been interesting

before. I waited to see what he would say next.

"And, of course, what's interesting about it, as I'm sure you're aware, is that it's changed. I detect a new pattern in what you're doing at the moment."

"Yes, sir?"

"Yes. When you started here your work was pretty much what we'd expect from a lad of your age. Not brilliant but certainly up to the mark. But now it's become, well, how shall I put it...?"

"Interesting?"

"Useless, I think is the word I want."

"Useless?"

"Yes, it's useless. No good."

"Is it?"

"Let's take a look at this piece for example."

He tossed a book at me across the desk.

"What's wrong with it, sir?"

"It's upside down for one thing."

"Is it, sir? I didn't realize."

"Oh, I think you did, Gordon. Just examine it a moment. Refresh you memory. Apart from the fact that it's on the correct page and more or less employs the alphabet, there's nothing right about it."

He lifted his eyebrows and peered at me for a moment. I offered him a worried frown, but somehow he detected that it was a fake.

"I shouldn't be too smug about it, Gordon. You see, I believe I know what your game is."

"Game, sir?"

"It's all this average business, isn't it?"

"Is it?" I asked.

"I've had a word with Miss Cassidy. It was in her lesson that it all started, wasn't it?"

"She did say something about averages, sir, yes."

"The thing is you're *trying* to be different, just to show you're not average. That won't do. Anyway, it's too easy. Just making a botch of things doesn't prove anything."

"Mr Peck told us there couldn't be an average person, sir. He said it was impossible."

"Well, it's not impossible, I suppose, but it's highly unlikely. From what I've heard no one's yet proved that you're *not* average. Which is very interesting. Have you thought about it like this before? The really average person, if he exists, could actually decide what the rest of us think and do."

"No. I hadn't thought about it like that."

"It's quite fascinating. One person who, without realizing it, influences the habits and behaviour of everyone he comes in contact with. If this is the case, Gordon," he said, tapping my book, "you can see the difficulty it presents, can't you?"

"Can I, sir?"

"Hand in rubbish like this and they'll all be turning out rubbish soon. Following your trend. What concerns me is your academic work. The educational standards of the whole school – indeed, the whole country – could plummet if people begin to follow your lead. And we don't want that, do we?"

He was still smiling, trying to make light of it all. I shrugged. He might not have wanted it, but at that moment I couldn't have cared less.

"I want you to know that I appreciate the way you feel. And that I have a suggestion to make. It's rather unconventional, but I think it will help."

He went over to a cupboard in the corner of the room and pulled out Miss Cassidy's dummy. I wasn't expecting that.

"I think you've seen this before, haven't you?" he said, heaving the dummy into a spare chair.

"Yes."

"It represents the average pupil, doesn't it? And I think you've come to identify with it. You see the dummy as an extension of yourself. Perhaps you've never quite put it into words but it's there somewhere, lodged in your head."

I didn't know what to say. We sat looking at the slumped dummy for a moment or two.

"What are you thinking?" he asked eventually.

I was thinking he'd probably flipped and I might have to make a break for it at any moment, but I didn't say so. Instead I said,

"Perhaps you're right, sir."

"And how are you feeling towards this dummy?"

"Erm..."

"I mean, do you like it?"

"Not particularly."

"No. Of course you don't. In fact you hate it, don't you? You hate it because it stands for a part of you which you would rather didn't exist."

"Do I, sir?"

"Yes. Let me put my suggestion to you. And you are at liberty to refuse, Gordon. It is only a suggestion. I recommend that you take this dummy down to the gym, when nobody else is about, and you beat the living daylights out of it."

"I see, sir."

"Get it out of your system. All this business about being average. Take it out on the dummy. No one will see you do it. You can then come out of the gym a new man. No need to try and be different again. The dummy, your average self, will be defeated and only the real Gordon Nesbitt will be left."

"Well..."

"Of course, I'm assuming the dummy won't win," he chortled. "What do you think? Will you give it a try?"

Brains: *Nesbitt's Winning Ways*

It seemed to me I'd been getting it wrong all these years. My ploy had always been to look a little bit hard, know the ropes, talk smooth and easy and, well, the rest of it. You couldn't set out an exact formula for women, but after a while you absorbed a method and you just *knew* how it worked. A mix of charm and experience and psychology. But along came Nesbitt and turned all that on its head.

The answer was *not* to know what you're doing. The answer was to be a natural born prat and the women would buzz round you like bees. I know, it sounds mad, but I had it from the horse's mouth, as they say, and the horse in this case was none other than Lorraine "the Lips" Bartlett of the fourth year. A friendly sort of girl and much sought after. Also rather tasty and very well-spoken with a voice warm enough to melt butter. I was walking home when she caught up with me and said she had something to tell me about my friend Nesbitt.

I didn't specially want to hear. Everyone had something to say about him and I was getting a shade cheesed off with it. But I humoured her. After all, walking home with Lorraine was better than a hot sausage up your nose any day of the week.

"So what is this Nesbitt info, Lorraine?" I asked.

She told me that she'd just seen Nesbitt mooching along by the hedge at the bottom of the field. Well away from other people.

"Hello, Gordon," she'd said.

He'd looked at her but hadn't answered. She'd placed herself in front of him so he couldn't avoid her eyes. Then she'd reached up and kissed him.

"You what?" I said.

"There wasn't anyone about."

"Yes, but..."

"And I wanted to know."

"Wanted to know? Wanted to know what?"

"I wanted to know what it was like. I mean, he's your average bloke, isn't he?"

"That's what they say, but..."

"So I wanted to know what the average bloke kisses like."

"My God."

"Only for purposes of comparison. It didn't mean anything."

"I'm glad to hear it. What did he do?"

"He blinked."

"I should think he would. Is that all?"

"I think he was about to kiss me back, actually. He looked a bit as if he didn't know where he was, but I think that's what was in his mind."

"And?"

"Nothing."

"Nothing?"

"There was a rustling further down the hedge and it put him off. Then he went bright red and beetled off as fast as he could."

"What a fool."

"It didn't matter. I found out what I wanted to know."

I was trying to fit all the pieces of this weird picture together as she began to turn off down her street. It wasn't easy. I kept seeing Noddy, face all red, running away with his head down.

"Hang on a minute," I said to Lorraine. "If you're so keen to know, how about ... I mean, why don't you ... you and me..."

"No thanks, Brains," she said with a smile. "I'm not that curious."

And she went, still smiling.

Nesbitt: Learning How to Run

"You've stopped talking about the Dumb Blonde," said Colin on our evening run.

In fact I'd stopped talking about everything. We'd walked to the river in silence and I'd run to the last boat house and back before either of us spoke. I think I wanted to talk but hardly knew where to begin. I certainly wasn't going to tell

Colin about Lorraine. No point being scoffed at by a dog when you can avoid it.

I couldn't work that little incident out at all. I was taking the long way home, by the hedge at the bottom of the field. I thought I was alone, which was what I wanted, but, all of a sudden, Lorraine was standing there in front of me with a soft smile on her face. I don't think she said anything. She might've done; I can't remember because I was so stunned by what happened next. She stepped up and kissed me. This is a girl who'd hardly spoken to me before. And not a bad-looking one either. I wish I'd known it was coming so I could have appreciated it a bit better. The way it happened it was over before I knew. Like a slap round the face. She stepped back and looked at me, as if she was studying me. To see what I'd do next, I suppose. My first thought was that this was a massive piss-take. Brains and the others were probably lurking around somewhere, sniggering in their hands. And Jackie was probably there too, camera at the ready. Then I thought, sod it, I don't care. I'll kiss her back. Give them something to snigger about. Part of me wanted to anyway. But just as I was about to do that, I saw these faces in the hedge. Not Brains or Jackie, but a couple of second years, Jo Corduroy and Sean James. With notebooks. Bloody hell, it gave me a turn. I felt like some kind of endangered species being watched by a couple of midget David Attenboroughs. So I legged it. I don't know if they'd set Lorraine up or not – I was too confused to work it out – but I wish it hadn't happened.

This is not the kind of thing you chat over with

people. Even with Colin. I did think about mentioning Madge's dummy suggestion but decided against that too. Alsopp obviously thought I was off my trolley and if I told Colin about it he just might agree.

"She's still around, is she?" said Colin.

"Claire? Yes, I think so."

"But you haven't seen her?"

"Yes, I've seen her."

"Ah."

"What do you mean by 'ah'? You sound like a psychiatrist."

"I just mean 'ah, so you've seen her, but you only *think* she's still around.'"

"So?"

"So," he said, yawning, "it sounds as if you're pretending you don't care whether you've seen her or not when, in fact, you do."

"Oh, do I?"

"Probably. Is she still pretty?"

"I don't know."

"No?"

"Yes, I suppose she is."

"Yes?"

"Yes, she's pretty. She looks lovely. What's that got to do with it?"

"Quite a lot. I've seen it before, Gordon. This sort of confusion in the young."

"The young?" I said. "Don't give me that balls, Colin. How can you go on about me being young when you're only seven."

"Seven dog years, which makes me mature enough, I think."

113

"Oh, yes. Middle-aged. Getting on even..."

"Please, Gordon. If you carry on like that you'll only depress me."

"Then that'll make two of us, won't it?"

"Ah."

"And don't start that again."

And that was the end of the conversation. The walk ended as it had begun – in silence. There was nothing else to talk about as far as I was concerned. Colin wanted to talk about Claire and I didn't. That's all there was to it.

I felt very dissatisfied with myself as we made our way back to the house. For one thing I hadn't trained properly. I should've run further and put more into it. I wondered whether my heart was still in the race. Was I beginning to give up the idea of doing well? Just accepting that I wasn't up to much so I might as well not bother?

We crossed the bridge to the main road, and in a sudden fit of frustration I started running again, dragging Colin along behind me. I knew that I'd jerked the lead without warning him, that I was probably hurting him, but I didn't care. Colin skidded along the pavement for a few strides and then broke into a lolloping run as he tried to keep up. I pulled on the lead and pressed on faster.

Minutes of the Fourth Meeting of the Normal Nesbitt Fan Club

Fifteen full members present, plus a number of interested observers. The winner of the observation competition was M. de Beere, who noted the following facts:

Gordon Nesbitt has a dog that he walks by the river most evenings. He also runs, probably in training for the Halliwell Bowl.

His mother works in a newsagent's in town.

His sister is called Jeanette and is appearing in *Twelfth Night* with a drama group in July. (Those members who are not on holiday will attend a performance of this.)

He has a brother called Stuart who goes to Radford Road Primary.

He was born in Wolverhampton (the Midlands!) but moved from there when he was three.

He has had at least three meetings with Mr Alsopp so far this term.

There were other facts, but most members also had those. For a full list see the club scrapbook.

S. James and J. Corduroy gave an account of some interesting Nesbitt-spotting done after school last week. This was about the famous Lorraine Bartlett incident which most people seem to know about by now. W. Faber (new member) proposed that the Normal Nesbitt Fan Club should follow Lorraine

Bartlett's example, but there were heated protests about this, led by F. Whale. He said that the L.B. incident was really an example of L.B.'s behaviour, not Nesbitt's, so we shouldn't take too much notice of it. If we all started copying things that happened to N.N. we would have to break our legs if he happened to break his leg, catch colds when he caught colds and so on. The meeting agreed that this didn't make much sense. However, it was decided to hold a new competition based on things Nesbitt might do. J. Corduroy suggested dog-walking but M. de Beere pointed out that this wasn't competitive and, anyway, where were we going to get the right kind of dogs from? F. Whale and M. de Beere were asked by the meeting to select some Nesbitt-type act that *could* be included in a competition.

(M. de B.)

Alsopp: *Memo to Self*

As far as I can tell Gordon Nesbitt has not taken me up on the dummy idea. This is disappointing since I'm sure it would help. It would help both of us actually. It would help him by exorcizing this peculiar obsession about being average, and it would help me by tying up a loose end. God knows I've got enough on my plate without worrying whether Nesbitt is going to go a couple of rounds with a stuffed dummy.

Another worrying aspect of the affair is the effect it's beginning to have on the staff. Ron Peck, for example. So I'm told, he's gathered together all the statistics on Nesbitt he can find and he's feeding them into a computer. Well, all right, he's got a mathematical mind and this kind of thing is likely to interest him. But he's beginning to neglect his other duties. He's rarely seen in the staff room these days and someone told me he's losing weight and looking rather haunted. So what am I to do about that? Have him in for a chat? Suggest he biffs a model of Gordon Nesbitt around?

Running a school this size is like running a business. We have a considerable turnover. However, every time I try to switch my attention to the administration of the establishment, I find myself drifting off and wondering about *him*. What's he up to now? Where is he? What will he do next?

Brains: *Nesbitt Goes Out on a Limb*

I wouldn't have minded all that attention myself, but poor old Noddy couldn't cope with it. Everyone knew who he was. All heads turned to look when he went by. Even the staff started getting his name right. Half the Lower School belonged to Miranda de Beere's Normal Nesbitt Fan Club. She's a batty young thing, always organizing her cronies to do something daft. Usually people let her get on with it and tell her to buzz off if she comes too close. This time, though, she had an amazing following, all dead keen to find out more and more about little Noddy.

And what about little Noddy himself? Well, he

wasn't happy about it. Maybe it was because no one actually spoke to him much. They looked at him, watched him like hawks, but they didn't speak to him. Of course, that wasn't very different from the way it always was, but it had never bothered him before. Now he was looking as if he was on his own. The barriers were up.

I went into lunch one day and saw him sitting by himself near a window and staring out across the tarmac. It looked as if the bodily Nesbitt was there, chewing miserably at a plate of salad, but the real person wasn't, somehow. Off with the fairies or something. I took my tray and sat down next to him. He hadn't heard me coming and he jumped when I slid my knife and fork on the table. But he didn't say anything. Instead he stood up and started to clear away his plate of salad.

"Don't go," I said. "I only just sat down."

"Is that any reason to stay?"

He needed something to cheer him up. A change of gear. Take his mind off all this unwelcome attention he was getting.

"Look, I've got something to show you."

For a moment he stood there, wondering whether to walk off, but the force of my open personality made him hesitate. He sighed and sat down. I gave him an encouraging, warm smile and patted the breast pocket of my jacket.

"You want to see what I've got here?" I asked, looking about to make sure we weren't being watched.

"No."

"You will when you know what it is." I slid a

white paper bag across the table at him. "Don't let anyone see it."

Nesbitt: More Trouble With Photographs

There was a fan of white borders on shiny card at the opening of the bag. I groaned. The Brains Boob Collection. What did he take me for?

"Oh, come on, Brains," I said. "I'm not in the mood for photos."

"No," he said. "It's all right. They're decent. Take a look."

Holiday snaps, I thought. Views of his mum and dad leaning sideways and smiling, with the tops of their heads cut off; Brains on the beach trying to tan his spindly body and look cool. Not what I'd call decent. I pulled one of the photos out and glanced down at it. It wasn't a holiday snap.

"See?" said Brains. "Not bad, eh?"

"Where did you get these?" I asked, sliding them out and spreading them on the table.

"Jackie. She made some copies for me. What do you think?"

It was Claire, in her tracksuit, swinging her arms; then standing with Brains and looking at the watch; running, with her hair swept up off her face.

Brains leaned over and selected one of the pictures with the tip of his fingers. He lowered his voice.

"Look at that. The way she holds herself. Fantastic. She's going to have a good few inches on

Metson if they come to the tape together, isn't she?"

I was dumb-struck for a while, feeling irritable and cheap and yet, at the same time, fascinated by the pictures.

"Why show me?" I asked at length.

"Why do you think? Because I knew you'd like them."

"I never said that..."

"Oh, no. You never *said*. You didn't have to. I know you, Noddy."

"No, you don't."

"There's nothing to be ashamed of. We agreed, she's a real looker. She's made to be looked at."

"Does she know you've got these?"

"What do you think?" he said with a snort. "I can get you copies if you like. Twenty-five p—"

"No."

"You can pay me tomorrow—"

"No!"

He shrugged and started to put the photos back into the paper bag. I watched them go, Claire's perfect face slipping into his grubby pocket.

"Why don't you grow up, Baines?" I said.

"What?"

"When are you ever going to stop being a small-minded kid?"

"Look, I only thought..."

"Oh, leave it out. You only thought. Don't make me laugh, because you never think. It's beyond you. You're pathetic, Baines."

Snatching up my plate I turned my back and marched off. I looked back at him just once before

120

I left the hall. He hadn't moved from the table and was staring at me with open eyes like a cat that's just been shown the door.

I went running alone that night, without bothering to take Colin. I burned along the river bank faster than ever before. I went well beyond the last boat house this time, forging on and on until I could go no further. A good, clean run, fuelled again by the heat of this anger that I couldn't properly understand. It was as if each pounding step was clearing my mind, making life simpler to live. Not thinking or worrying; just running. Pure running without thought. My heart pumped the energy, and my head remained empty.

When I did stop I felt no elation. I realized that although I'd been fast I had also used up all my strength. And that wasn't good enough. I had to cover a greater distance. It was no good running fast on hatred and coming to a standstill short of the distance. The hatred had to go into the planning of the race as much as it went into the running.

The light was fading from the sky as I sat down on the river bank and rested. I watched a couple of ducks paddling aimlessly around below me. A single oarsman pulled past on his way upstream. He cut through the water with a great, steady control, grim-faced, not even seeing me. That's the way I had to do it. With control, paying out the distance as if it was a coil of rope coming from inside me.

After I'd rested I walked on for twenty minutes

or so and then turned round to begin the run back.

When I got home I heard the telly in the front room and Dad's low voice muttering to Mum. I crept upstairs. I didn't want to speak to anyone, especially them. At the top of the stairs I paused to listen. Apart from the tinny sounds from the telly the house was quiet. Dad couldn't be heard any more. Maybe he was staring at the screen, or maybe he'd slipped out. The place might almost have been empty.

Stuart's door was slightly ajar – he liked to have the light from the landing spilling into his room. I pushed the door open a little and looked in. He was asleep; a still mound under his gaudy duvet, his thick head sunk in the pillow. My gormless brother. There was a little pile of cars on the floor beside the bed, all carefully arranged, and a comic had slipped out of his hand on top of them. How long was it since I'd fallen asleep reading comics? I sort of envied him.

Brains: *The Horrible Truth About Nesbitt*

I am a tolerant man. I can put up with all manner of weirdos. Even after Nesbitt lashed out at me I thought, well, he's under pressure. It's nothing personal. Time will pass and he'll apologize. I'm easy-going like that. But you have to draw the line somewhere. Sometimes you have to stop in your tracks and say, sorry but this is just not on. It's unacceptable and I'm not having anything to do with it.

So it was with Nesbitt. After what I saw in the gym there was only one thing to be said.

Nesbitt was sick.

He'd taken to beetling off home by himself with a face like yesterday's fish. OK, I thought. It's your choice. You don't want to speak to people, don't expect to have a flock of friends round when the chips are down. It's give and take in this life. Suit yourself, pal.

Then, one afternoon, he didn't shoot off. He skulked around waiting for everyone else to go. It was obvious to me. I mean, Nesbitt is transparent when he's up to something. He hasn't got the first idea about being furtive.

I got curious so I left as usual, hung around for ten minutes and doubled back. There was a game of rounders on the field and I was tempted to stay and watch, but the thought of Nesbitt plotting something in some empty room lured me away. I did the full circuit of the upper and lower corridors and saw no sign of him. Then I caught sight of a movement in the gym and sure enough, there he was. All by himself. Well, I thought he was all by himself. He's putting in a bit of training for the race, I thought. So he does care after all. He's afraid he's going to flop so he's doing a few exercises. Alone. I was on the brink of feeling sorry for him.

Then I crept round the outside of the gym to the PE store door and sneaked a look. You could get into the store and see through the frosted glass window into the gym. It distorted the image a bit, but, my God, I could see all too clearly what

Nesbitt was up to. I can tell you it wasn't just the image that was distorted.

For a start he wasn't alone. He had a little kid with him. It must have been one of his precious fan club – Miranda's loonies who dress themselves up to look like him – because I could see the kid had these brightly-coloured odd socks on. He was slumped against the wall bars and Nesbitt was talking to him.

"OK, what have you got to say for yourself?" he said.

The kid was too scared to answer. I'm sure I heard him whimpering.

"I see," Nesbitt went on. His voice was icy cold, harder than I'd ever heard it before. "You think it's funny to take the piss, do you?"

Was he so thick? Taking the piss? Couldn't he see that kids like this one *admired* him? They wanted to be like him. God knows why, but they did. Oh yes, they could be a bloody nuisance and they'd got on his nerves all right, but that didn't mean he had to take them aside and frighten the life out of them, did it?

"You know what I think of people like you? You're nothing. You don't even exist. A miserable blank. And you make me want to throw up."

I mean, this is the way to talk to an admirer, is it?

"You brainless bastard!"

And he hit him. He took a vicious swipe and sent the kid sprawling. I saw his pale legs twist with the pain and then he lay quite still. Good God, I thought. What the hell's got into Nesbitt here?

Then he hit him again. He knelt down and punched him in the stomach. I winced and turned my head away. I thought I was going to be sick on the spot. What should I do? Nesbitt was going berserk in that gym. He could do some serious damage the way he was carrying on.

"I've had about all I can take from snot-bags like you. Take that! And that!"

Now he was kicking him! I looked through the window again and he was kicking the poor little body senseless. It lifted in the air and clumped to the gym floor with a sickening thud. Then Nesbitt stopped and looked up, like an animal at the kill. Voices came drifting in from outside. The rounders girls were on their way in. Nesbitt grabbed his unconscious victim by the ankles and started dragging him towards the PE store.

That was the strangest sight – the way he dragged that kid by the ankles, as if he was pulling a wheelbarrow or something. It's not the sort of thing you forget. I was frozen to the spot by it. Frozen until a sudden sound made me move again, that is. It wasn't Nesbitt and it wasn't the rounders girls. Someone else was snooping about. Someone else had witnessed Nesbitt's vile attack.

Well, there wasn't much I could do about it now. In fact, in that kind of mood, with a horrible mad strength, Nesbitt would probably go for me too. No. The only thing to do in those circumstances was to clear off as fast as I could. And that's what I did.

Minutes of the Fifth Meeting of the Normal Nesbitt Fan Club

? members present. (S. James was appointed as a teller, but he spent the entire meeting counting heads without coming up with the same number twice. We'll just say that we had a full house.) Business was concentrated on the Normal Nesbitt competition (part two). M. de Beere and F. Whale explained and read out the rules.

Explanation: Gordon Nesbitt was observed (by M. de Beere) in the school gym. He was seen in combat with an unidentified opponent. What he did was to take his opponent by surprise, pull him down and drag him for several metres over the floor by his ankles. To quote our observer: "I only saw him for a moment, but his actions were very quick and completely successful." This is what we have isolated as the most interesting bit of Nesbitt behaviour so far and our competition is based on it.

Rules:

i) Members should form into teams of two or three.

ii) Over the next two weeks the teams should try to knock down and drag backwards as many victims as they can.

iii) This is to be called the Nesbitt Rush and will only count if it has been witnessed by at least two non-team members, entered on a sheet and dated.

iv) No injured or sick person to be selected as a victim. The knock-down should be clean and effected by surprise rather than violence.

v) Teams found to be informing victims before-hand, or entering into agreements with victims, will be disqualified.

vi) Points to be scored according to the status of the victims, as follows: first years – 1 point each; second years – two points each; third years – four points each; Upper School females – eight points each; Upper School males – ten points each; members of staff – fifteen points each; heads of department – 1, 2 or 3 bonus points, depending who (e.g. Mr Holloway – 3 bonus points; Miss Cassidy – 1 bonus point); visitors, domestic staff, postmen etc. – no score.

vii) No victim to be selected more than once.

viii) Closing date – the day of the Halliwell Bowl.

(M. de B.)

Alsopp: *Memo to Self*

Thank goodness that's over. Saw Nesbitt for what I hope will be the last time. The fight with his *alter ego* (the dummy) has at last taken place and must be considered a tremendous success. A simple device, really, but the world's best ideas are simple. As I showed Gordon out I was convinced that he looked more relaxed and at peace with himself than he has done before. The boy is cured and I can't help feeling that I have done some good. Hard for head teachers to make that claim most of the time, but in this case I feel it's perfectly justified.

Had a small sherry to celebrate.

"Well, Gordon, did you take up my little suggestion?" Alsopp said to me in the quiet of his room.

"Yes, sir."

"And?"

"Well ... I did as you said..."

"Yes?"

I wasn't sure what he wanted. A blow by blow account? How I felt?

("I felt like a wally, sir. I knew I would and I did. Thanks very much, sir, but I suppose it takes a practised wally like yourself to think up such a piss-awful idea.")

"I won, sir."

"Good, good," he laughed, banging the flat of his hand on his desk. Enjoying the joke. "And how do you feel now?"

Yes, how did I feel now? I hadn't thought about it much.

"Normal, sir."

"Normal? Splendid. I thought you would. I thought it would get it out of your system."

("But normal is exactly how I felt before, you utter pillock, sir. Normal is how I *don't* want to feel.")

"May I go, sir?"

"Of course, of course. Do feel you can pop in if there's anything you want to chat over, won't you?"

"Yes, sir, thank you, sir."

And I backed out and closed the door behind

128

me. I thought I could still hear him chortling to himself as I went off to find the rest of my group.

I asked myself the question again: How do you feel? Normal? I felt dull and heavy. Life was taking a long curve into a flat, flat landscape with no distinguishing marks. Nothing by the roadside. Nothing on the horizon. I felt rotten.

Brains: *A Problem Shared*

The business of Nesbitt suddenly turning into a homicidal maniac was getting me down. After all, now he had the taste for it he might go for someone else. It's like tigers. Once they get a mouthful of human meat, no amount of Whiskas or tasty cat biscuits is enough for them. What they want is Man, red and raw and fresh. Nesbitt could attack again. Maybe even those he thought were closest to him.

I must admit that the thought of Nesbitt suddenly sinking his fangs into my neck or something began to get me down. My mind wasn't always on what I was doing. For example, one morning I was working on the Humanities project – Operation Nesbitt we called it now – and I noticed that Jackie and I were the only two in the room. (Well, there were three actually, but as the other one was Miss Cassidy and she was warbling away to herself in one corner, we were effectively on our own.) Jackie's not a bad person to be working with at close quarters. She's a girl who's entitled to expect your full attention. And what was I thinking about? Nesbitt the Ripper. So something was wrong, wasn't it?

"All this average stuff," I said to her. "What do you make of it?"

"I make images of it," she said. "Photographs."

"I don't mean that. I mean Nesbitt. Do you think he's really average, like they say?"

"I suppose he must be. All the evidence points to it."

"Not all the evidence."

"No?"

"No. I've got evidence to point to the fact that he's extremely un-average."

She pricked up her ears at that. Chance of an unusual snap or something, I suppose.

"Tell me more," she said.

"Average people don't go in for heavy violence, do they?"

"Heavy violence? Nesbitt?"

"I know it's hard to believe, but I've seen it with my own eyes."

And I described what I'd witnessed in the gym. She found it hard to believe.

"So where's the victim, Brains? If Nesbitt's done what you say, there should be some little kid knocking around with bandages and stuff all over him."

"Unless he's off school," I said. "Too sick and frightened to turn up. And I'm the only one who knows about it. You know what that means?"

"What?"

"I'm a target, aren't I? It also puts me in a pretty responsible position. I have to do something about it."

Miss Cassidy came trilling over to see what we

were doing. Lovely pictures, Jackie. Super. Such movement, such composition. Etc etc. Trill, trill. In her element because there was so much interest in Operation Nesbitt.

"I don't suppose that either of you has seen my dummy, have you?" she asked brightly. "Mr Alsopp borrowed it for a while, but he said he'd return it."

"What did he want it for?" asked Jackie.

"I don't know. I guess he's interested in the Project. But we'll need it back in time for the presentation, won't we?"

"Maybe we won't," said Jackie. "Maybe we can use a blow-up of Gordon Nesbitt instead."

"An inflatable, you mean?"

"No, no. A blow-up photo. I've got a couple of good shots here, and if Nesbitt's our average pupil..."

"Seems a shame not to make use of the dummy, though, Jackie. It took a lot of preparation..."

"I could do you a life-size face to stick on it if you like."

"Give it a face? Hmm. That could be good. What sort of face?"

"Nesbitt."

I sighed out loud. All this chitchat about dummies when lives were at stake.

"I think I saw the dummy in the craft store, Miss Cassidy," I said. "I'm not sure, but I think it was there."

"Really? Then perhaps I should pop along to look."

And off she went, singing away to herself, daft as a brush.

"What's it doing in the craft store, Brains?" Jackie asked.

"Nothing. It's not there as far as I know. I only said that to get rid of her."

She narrowed her eyes at me as if to say, what's your game here? Trying to fix it so we're alone? But she didn't look too fierce about it and in normal circumstances it would've been a fair ploy. My mind was not on entanglements with Jackie Maugham, though. Pity, but there you are. While Nesbitt was on the prowl I had to set aside thoughts like that.

"Look, I've got to do something about this," I said. "We've got to do something."

"We? It's nothing to do with me."

"It is now. I've told you about it."

"OK, then. I'll see what I can find out. I reckon you're wrong, but I'll sniff around and see what turns up. A little bit of investigative journalism. Fair enough?"

"And what am I going to do?"

"Well, if you think it's that serious, you should go and see Madge about it."

"Madge? Are you kidding?"

"Not if you're right. Tell Madge what you saw. He'd love to hear about it."

I think she thought I wouldn't do it.

"Right," I said. "I will. That's what I'll do. See Madge."

And I did. In the first break I went along and tapped on his door and he summoned me in to his Holy Chamber, where he sat behind his desk, beaming at me like a bank manager.

"And what's all this about, Trevor?" he asked, pressing the tips of his fingers together and looking at me over the top of them.

"It's about Nesbitt, sir."

"Ah, yes. I think things have taken a turn for the better, don't you?" he said.

"The better?" I echoed. "You think it's better?"

"Well, Gordon seems very much more himself, wouldn't you say?"

"More himself?"

"Yes. He's sorted things out, I believe."

"Do you, sir? Do you really?"

"Trevor, if you're simply going to turn my statements into questions we're not going to get anywhere. What are you getting at?"

He really had no idea. There he was, beaming away behind his desk and thinking he'd got it all sorted out, while Nesbitt was outside somewhere, probably kicking hell out of some little kid at that very moment.

"You've really got no idea, have you, sir?" I said.

"Not until you tell me, no."

"Then I'll tell you."

"Please."

"I witnessed ... I saw with my own eyes..."

"Yes?"

"Nesbitt."

"Is that it?"

"I'm finding this hard to put into words, sir."

He slid a cuff off his watch and glanced down.

"I have a meeting at two, Trevor."

"In the gym, sir. I saw Nesbitt in the gym..."

"Ah."

"You'll never believe what he was doing."

"I think perhaps I will," he said, the smile returning. "He was having a fight."

"A fight? You call it a fight?"

"Trevor. Please. Don't start on the questions again."

"I'm sorry, sir, but I would not call what I saw a fight."

"Well, strictly speaking I suppose it wasn't..."

He knew about it. And this was the man who liked to keep control of things, who was supposed to stand for law and order.

"I can't believe you know about it, sir. You just couldn't stay so calm if you really knew."

"Well I do know," he said, "because it was my idea."

"What?"

"My idea. I suggested it to Gordon myself."

"My God."

"I thought it would work some of this suppressed anger out of him and, I have to say, I think I was right."

"That is sick, sir," I said. Straight talking to a man like Madge, but I couldn't help it. I'm not the sort to flinch from the truth. "I'm sorry to say so, but that is sick."

"No, Trevor. It's not sick. It's unconventional, perhaps. But not sick. The fact that Gordon feels better about himself proves the point."

"I can't believe I'm hearing this. So Nesbitt feels better so everything is all right?"

"I've got the measure of Gordon now. I understand him at last. This is the point..."

"Excuse me, Mr Alsopp. I have to be going," I said and I left. I turned my back on him and walked calmly – well, fairly calmly – out of the room.

I'd gone there to tell him what I'd seen. To see what should be done about it. A couple of responsible adults talking things over for the sake of the common good. I never expected to find that it was all Alsopp's idea. "Not feeling too well, Gordon? What a shame. Try beating up some weedy first year. You'll feel much better after that." Is this what he tells everyone? "Worried about those exam results? Try kicking in a head or two. It'll perk you up no end." He must've had a real binful of maniac ideas stashed away under that sensible hair-cut of his.

I'd seen that kind of thing on enough films to know that I wasn't safe in his room. The bloke you think you can trust the most is the one who is most likely to do you in. Men in suits with smarmy voices, just like him, dancing about in the woods with white robes on and stabbing goats. But if I couldn't trust our noble Head, who could I trust? I mean, what was happening to this school?

Nesbitt: A Glimmer of Hope

I was by myself in the kitchen, washing up. Almost by myself. Colin had settled into his basket in the corner. He was treading round in a slow circle, making the most of the fact that we weren't going out for a run. The race was too close. A day to go. I was better off saving my energy and concentrating my mind and the only place where I could do that was the kitchen.

The others were stuck in front of the telly and Jeanette had flounced out to a rehearsal. She was playing the part of an armchair or something in some weird thing Justin had written for their group. Jeanette reckoned it was very exciting because it had no people in it, only household objects, and no one knew exactly how it was going to turn out. Like life itself, she said. Well, it was true that Justin didn't know how things were going to turn out, because Jeanette was about to give him the elbow and fix her fangs on some other poor oik. She uses that drama group like a library; once she's been through one man she hands him in and takes out another. Sometimes I expect to see them with a date stamped on their foreheads. And they meekly put up with it. They never seem to complain. That's one of the things that gets me about Jeanette. She controls what happens to her. She doesn't do what she doesn't want to do. Why aren't I like that? Why can't I make things happen? It's true that things had been happening lately, but they were way beyond my control.

"Mind you," I told Colin, "it's not just me. The whole place is getting out of control."

"Has it ever been otherwise?" said Colin.

"I mean, this is weird. They've started dragging each other round on their bums."

"Really?"

"Yes. It's stupid."

"Who are we talking about, Gordon?"

"Some of the younger kids. It's a sort of craze.

They crawl around on their hands and knees, grab someone by his ankles, pull him over and drag him along on his bum. It's mad."

"I see."

"Why should they do a thing like that?"

Colin clacked his jaws on a biscuit and thought.

"To me it sounds like the sort of behaviour they've copied from someone," he said. "That's very often how these silly trends start."

"Yes, but who would be weird enough to do a thing like that?"

"I'm afraid you're asking rather a lot of me if you expect me to justify the ways of man to man, Gordon."

"You know what bugs me?" I said. "They tell me I'm the average example of this lot. And they're dragging people round on their bums. So what sort of a person does that make me?"

"Well, it could mean they're wrong, couldn't it? If you can't understand them doing things like that, it could be that you're not average after all."

"You could be right, Colin. You could be right about that."

Suddenly Colin had provided me with a glimmer of hope. It could be that I was getting things out of proportion. After all, if everyone was following my example, you wouldn't call them weird, would you? You'd call them dull or something.

"Confident?" asked Colin suddenly.

"What?"

"About the race? Are you confident?"

"Yes," I said. "I think I am. I think a few people are going to be surprised tomorrow."

The first I knew about it was when I suddenly felt this pressure round my ankles. It was a faint sensation, as if I'd just remembered that I'd left cycle clips on. Then it tightened and the cycle clips turned into the grip of a torturer's leg-irons.

"What the hell..." I began, but before I could say another word my ankles had been whipped from under me and I was crashing to the ground. I landed with a jarring thump and found myself staring into the eyes of Miranda de Beere and Frank Whale. They were holding on to an ankle each and I didn't like the look on their faces. I'm sure one of them was dribbling.

"Now look, lads," I said, "if this is some kind of a joke you'd better..."

But they took no notice. In fact I'm not even sure they heard what I was saying. Their eyes were staring and their faces fixed in a grin and suddenly they were dragging me backwards up the corridor. One moment I was sitting there trying to reason with them and the next I was whizzing along the corridor on my arse. Still in the sitting position. Whale and de Beere, with an ankle each, were galloping ahead like cart-horses.

I felt like a prime prat. Completely helpless. Without the faintest idea of where I was going or why. It didn't take long to find out. We went the length of the corridor and when we reached the entrance hall de Beere and Whale, with a final twang of my ankles, fell aside and I went twirling across the polished floor. I had the good sense to go into a sort of parachute roll, but all the same I couldn't stop myself cannoning into Madge's door.

"Come," said a muffled voice.

I didn't move. My arse was both hot and numb at the same time and I wasn't sure I could walk. I rolled to my knees and the door opened.

"What are you doing down there, Trevor?" asked Alsopp.

I couldn't begin to tell him. If he thought it was so smart for Nesbitt to beat up juniors, arse-dragging could very easily be his latest ploy to make jerks like de Beere and Whale feel comfortable with themselves. Get things out of their systems. Well, maybe that was all right for them, but my backside was feeling as if it had just been welded over and nothing was ever going to get out of *my* system again.

"Did you want something, Trevor?" Madge said in his more-than-patient voice.

"Not particularly, sir. I just happened to be passing."

"I think you'd better get to your feet and come in for a moment, don't you?"

So I did.

It transpired that my arse hadn't been the first to hit the deck that day. Five similar cases had come to Madge's attention. Five. What was going on? That's what our noble Head wanted to know.

"Well, I'm sorry, Mr Alsopp," I said, "but if you're prepared to let Nesbitt get away with what he's been doing, then you must expect..."

"I really don't know why that business has got you so worked up, Trevor. It was a simple piece of therapy designed to help Gordon out of an identity crisis. What we have here is a dangerous bout of hooliganism made worse by the fact that it is entirely mindless and without reason."

"That's as maybe," I said, "but it wouldn't surprise me to find that Nesbitt was behind it somewhere. Mindless hooliganism, you said. That's Nesbitt. Get hold of the culprits and turn the screws, sir. You'll see I'm right."

"Turn the screws, Trevor? What do you think this is, the K.G.B.?"

I didn't answer that one.

"I'll make a few enquiries, Trevor. And we'll see what turns up. I'd like to keep a low profile at this stage of proceedings. If there is something nasty going on I don't want to frighten it back into the woodwork."

What a wonderful approach to violence. Make a few enquiries. In the meantime I had to live every moment wondering when I was next going to get whipped up the corridor on my arse.

Still, I'd already blown Alsopp's cover so I didn't really expect much help from him. I took things into my own hands and nobbled Whale at lunch. He wasn't at all bothered about what he'd done.

"So you knew it was us?" he said.

"Of course I did."

"Hmm. We'll have to wear a disguise or something."

"You mean, you're going to do it again?"

"You needn't worry, Brains," he said. "You've been done once. It shouldn't happen again. If it does it won't count."

"Won't count for what?"

"Points."

"Points? You get points for it?"

I could hardly believe what I was hearing. It sounded as if Alsopp was behind it after all. Points for arse-dragging? He'd be having them up in front of a general assembly, giving out certificates.

"How much of this has been going on?" I asked.

"Me and Beery done you and we done Dawn," Whale boasted.

"You done Dawn?" I said. "What did she have to say about it?"

"We was gone before she knew we'd done her. That's half the point. You move in. Whack! On their bums. Pull 'em along and leave 'em. Most people don't realize what's going on. You happened to recognize us, Brains. One up to you."

"Thanks very much."

"Dawn was too busy trying to keep her legs covered up."

"What I'd like to know is why?"

"Me too. I mean, if it was Jackie's legs or Claire..."

"Whale!"

"Yes, Brains?"

"Why are you dragging people around on their bums?"

"It's the N.N.F.C., isn't it?"

"The N.N.F.C.?"

"The Normal Nesbitt Fan Club. I'm Secretary and de Beere's President. Her and me's one team. Sean James and Jo Corduroy's another. There's about ten in all. We have this points system. We get ten for you."

"My God."

"We've got three done already and..."

"Why?" I interrupted. "Why are you doing it?"

"It's the Nesbitt Rush, isn't it? It's what he does."

"Is it?"

"'Course it is. Come off it, Brains. You must know that."

And, of course, when I stopped to think about it, it made a kind of crazy sense. The N.N.F.C. I remembered hearing someone else in the gym when Nesbitt was doing his foul work. It must have been one of his stupid fan club. And they were doing the same thing all over the school. It made me feel very lonely. Whale and de Beere and their weird crew were sick. Alsopp was sick. Everyone was sick, sick, sick. Sickest of the lot was Nesbitt. He was the cause.

What could I do about it? I'd tried going to the top and had no joy. Maybe I should do a runner.

Minutes of the Sixth Meeting of the Normal Nesbitt Fan Club

Results of the Nesbitt Rush competition. An encouraging twenty-three teams took part in the event. Third was C. Howard, D. Tonge and T. Jenkins with a magnificent 84 points. There was a tie for first place between S. James and J. Corduroy, and M. de Beere and F. Whale. It is noted that both these teams (who scored 92 points) consist of founder members of the N.N.F.C.

There was a suggestion from the floor that there

should be a play-off between the two winning teams, allowing them one extra day in which to get points. Carried by a majority vote.

From the chair M. de Beere exhorted all members to turn out and give Normal Nesbitt full support in today's Halliwell Bowl.

(M. de B.)

Nesbitt: The Moment of Truth (Part One)

The day itself. The Big Day. I stood on a bench in the changing rooms, looking out of the little lift-up window, and felt slightly sick. The field was swarming with people. You couldn't tell spectators from officials or runners. Half the school seemed to have turned out to watch. I told myself that most of them had come to see Claire, or even Metson, but I knew that most of them wanted to see me.

Someone – probably Holloway – was bellowing into a megaphone, asking for all competitors to come to the start. I climbed down from the bench and took a couple of deep breaths. The changing rooms were empty – I was the last to leave. The familiar smell of old sweat and damp from the tiles in the showers filled my nostrils. I saw a single, greying plimsoll festering away in one of the shoe-racks. And there were the sports bags of the other competitors, stuffed with rolled towels and tubs of talcum powder. The place was close and comfortable now that the other runners had gone to jiggle around at the start.

Well, Holloway had said don't run. Brains, in his roundabout way, advised me against it. Even Colin didn't think much of the idea. But I knew better and I said I would run. There wasn't much I could do about it now but go outside and face the crowds.

Alsopp: *Memo to Self*

No sooner have I dealt with this worrying Nesbitt business than something else turns up to plague the life out of me. There is a peculiar form of violence spreading through the school. I suppose it is violence, though it's not the usual sort of violence. People are being pushed over and dragged along by their ankles before being dumped and abandoned. So far no one has been hurt, but the most worrying part of it is that it just doesn't make sense. There is no obvious motive for these attacks. The victims seem to be selected at random and across the whole age band. I cannot sleep properly with this going on in my school. It feels as if everything is flying apart at the seams.

It should be easy to trace this kind of thing and stamp it out, but it's just impossible to find out who is behind it. From the descriptions we've had it sounds as if there is a very large gang at work. In fact I sometimes wonder whether half the school is trying to knock over the other half. No one is paying much attention to the normal running of the school or, heaven forbid, to work. There is a general atmosphere of tension about the place, as if it would take just one spark to send the lot up in a flare of chaos. I keep turning this over in my mind and I'm sure it must be the work of one twisted individual – some evil inspiration which has got the rest of the goats following. I'd give my eye-teeth to know who it is. Stamp out the inspiration and I'll stamp out the plague; I'm damn sure I will.

What makes it all so bloody annoying is the fact that I've just sorted out Gordon Nesbitt. Now I'm beginning to suspect that he's the only normal person to be found on the premises.

Brains: *A View of the Race*

I moved among the gathered runners looking for Nesbitt. Wise to know exactly where he was, I thought. Hunk called the runners to the start and I began to think that he'd chickened out. That's often the way with homicidal maniacs – they lust after blood but they're cowards at heart. Then I saw him, stepping out of the changing rooms and into the sunlight. He came towards the throng on the field, blinking against the light, and immediately all heads turned his way.

"Here he is!" someone shouted. "Look! It's Normal Nesbitt. Over here."

Then some sniggering, and some cheering, seemed to swell and pass through the crowd.

"Good God," said someone else. "Look at his shorts."

Nesbitt's long khaki shorts flapped around his knees like flags. Jackie came craning forward pointing her camera at his legs. I saw Holloway's jaw drop as he caught sight of the shorts. He glowered at them as if they were a deliberate insult to the good name of the school. Perhaps they were, too. I wouldn't put it past a person like Nesbitt. This was supposed to be a deadly serious race and here was Nesbitt, looking like some heavy from an old black-and-white Tarzan movie.

"Wicked gear, Nesbitt!" a voice called out. "What do you keep up the legs? Your packed lunch?"

"Yeah, a couple of pickled onions," screeched a tiny girl at the front and there was general laughter.

For God's sake, I thought, get on with the race. The sooner he's out of sight the better.

Nesbitt must've felt the same, because when the gun went off he sprinted down the field like a rabbit. He'd only gone a dozen strides before he realized he was on his own.

"Wait for it, Nesbitt!" called the Hunk and an ironic cheer went up from the crowd. The gun had been for the girls' race which was starting halfway down the field. I could see them moving off in one large mass, their heads going up and down like clockwork. Nesbitt trotted in a small circle back to the starting line.

Holloway walked deliberately towards him, fixing him with his healthy stare.

"You're turning this into a farce, lad," he hissed. "I accept your right to be out here, but I will not have you make a mockery of the school. Any more funny tricks and you'll be disqualified."

Nesbitt: The Moment of Truth
(Part Two)

I wanted to become a piece of empty space; to be suddenly transported up to the privacy of the computer room or somewhere. Or maybe merged in with the thick of the watching crowd, shouting and jeering with the rest of them. The one thing I didn't want to be doing was running in baggy shorts in the Halliwell Bowl. But once Holloway's gun had gone (for the second time) that's exactly what I was doing.

After a couple of minutes, though, the complete humiliation of that false start began to work to my advantage. It made me angry. I was almost swelling with anger. Gordon Nesbitt, the Incredibly Normal Hulk. The muscles on my thighs didn't exactly burst the seams of my shorts – they'd have to be pretty massive to manage that – but I did start running. Running properly, I mean; like I had the other night – my heart white hot and my head empty.

Everyone was pretty much together as we streamed out of the gate at the bottom of the field and wheeled right, into the sun. Metson's head jogged along above everyone else's, about a dozen people in front of me. His ears were red with the sunlight coming through them, like indicators on a motorbike. He was looking good, but it was impossible to sort the real runners from the rest at that stage. By the time we reached the park, though, things had changed. We were no longer a group. We were a strung-out line. A bossy woman in a blazer – probably from one of the other schools – stood at the entrance to the park and ushered us in, swinging her arms like someone guiding airliners in to land.

"This way! This way!" she kept shouting, although once she'd directed the front-runners into the park there was no need for her to say anything. The rest just followed.

As we approached the lake, the first of the boys began to overtake the last of the girls. Metson was still ahead of me but still in sight, too. A patch of dark sweat had appeared between his shoulder blades. I fixed my eyes on it. At regular intervals it would disappear behind the churning arm of one of the intervening runners, but I kept it in my mind and stayed close to it. We swept past another marshal, a little kid with glasses and a plastic box tucked under his arm. Sandwiches, I supposed. He stood stock-still, pointing the way with a single finger.

I didn't really need marshals to tell me where to go. I knew the route pretty well: round the lake, through the wood, across the diagonal path and out of the other gate to the tree-lined avenue of posh houses on the edge of town. But the marshals did serve some purpose. I used them to record my progress. Each one I put behind me meant that another stage of the race had been conquered.

I had no idea how far up the field I was – there were still plenty of runners ahead of me – but I noticed that some people were stumbling from a run to a jog. I even passed some who'd slowed to a walk.

Brains: *Facing Up to the Beast*

I managed to wangle myself a marshalling job. Anything, I thought, to get away from that place for an afternoon.

After the start I bundled into Ron Peck's car with four others and we were dropped off at various points along the course. One of my aims was to check on Claire's progress; give her a bit of encouragement and maybe a few tips. Actually I was pretty confident that she'd win it easily, but I thought the sight of me on the course might just give her the morale boost to kick on even stronger.

I'd been at my post about ten minutes, I suppose, when who should come plodding up the road towards me but Normal Nesbitt himself. Hello, I thought. There's been some mistake. He shouldn't be here yet. Then the penny dropped. He'd cut off a few big corners somewhere. First violence, then deliberately naff shorts, and now cheating.

"What the hell are you doing here?" I said as he lumbered up.

I didn't mean to speak to him. In fact I swore to myself that never another word would pass from my lips to the ears of a degenerate turd like Nesbitt. He ploughed on towards me, his face set like stone. It was as if he couldn't see me.

Right, I thought, this is as good a chance as any to tell him what I think of him, so I ran alongside him for a moment or two. I gave no thought to my personal safety.

"You're a vicious bastard, Nesbitt," I puffed. "You're ... a mindless ... yob..."

149

But I couldn't stay level long enough to say much more. I'd never seen him looking like that before, and I don't just mean the shorts. His face was set, full of concentration and determination. He was sort of transformed. It was a very, very depressing sight. Even more so when I remembered that this was the person I'd once trusted. This hooligan in jungle trunks was the only bloke I'd ever told about Clacton.

Nesbitt: Yet More Moments of Truth

I thought the race would be my moment of truth. A chance to prove myself. Maybe that was so, but it turned out to be a bloody long moment. So it's not just one moment of truth, I thought, but lots of moments, all loosely strung together. One was when I saw for the first time what my shorts looked like and I had to go outside and face the crowds. Then there was the start of the race, and other moments almost every few steps along the route. Another came when I found that Brains was one of the marshals.

For a few seconds he ran alongside me, jab-bering with excitement and making no sense. Then he stopped running and suddenly he was whipped backwards and out of sight. It was like going past a telegraph pole in a train. I risked one glance over my shoulder. He was receding fast and waving his arms in circles, mouthing something I couldn't hear.

Someone eased past me at that point and I

realized that it was the first time I'd been overtaken by anyone. Metson could no longer be seen and I felt I was sliding back and that my legs were becoming weak. I was being drawn steadily back to my true place, well down the field. I put my head down and ground my teeth together.

Don't think. Run. Don't think. Run.

But there were lumps of thought there some-where inside my head. I didn't know what they were but I could feel them and I had to struggle to keep them down.

And then, ahead of me about two hundred metres down the avenue of trees, I saw a girl in a blue vest, running easily, her blonde hair whisking from side to side. And that got me running again.

I overtook my overtaker. The sunlight coming through the trees flicked by with a steady beat and I drew nearer and nearer. But I let her stay ahead. I didn't want to pull in front with a flashy, sideways smile only to cave in and be left behind. That would prove nothing.

The marshal halfway down the avenue was Holloway. He was propped against his bike at a neat little crossroads, jotting notes on a clipboard and looking very much in control of things. Typical of him.

"Don't worry, chaps. I can start this race *and* look after one of the check-points. No sweat."

As each runner drew level, he indicated briefly where they should turn by flapping out the flat of his hand penguin-fashion and went straight back to his notes without a glimmer of expression. I guessed that would change when he saw me run by.

No-hope Nesbitt, whom he'd asked to withdraw, up with his favourite. I couldn't wait to see his face.

But his face didn't change. He looked up, saw me and looked down again. If he felt any surprise he didn't show it. "Yes, Normal Nesbitt. Quick look at the watch. Tick the chart. Thanks very much. Next, please."

Without lifting his head he stuck one hand out to point the way.

And I took no notice and ran straight on.

I didn't plan it. I wasn't thinking. I just saw the flat of his hand and found myself ignoring it. In fact I brushed against it, causing him to spin round in a quarter circle and drop his clipboard.

"Nesbitt!" he bellowed after me. "Not that way, you fool! Turn left! Left!"

Minutes of an Emergency Meeting of the Normal Nesbitt Fan Club

Members present: M. de Beere, F. Whale, J. Corduroy and S. James. Purpose: to compare notes on the play-off for the Normal Nesbitt Rush competition. After a morning's work, both teams had notched up 7 more points. The fact that it was the day of the race made things particularly tricky. With so many people outside to see the start, it was easy enough to pull a victim over, but jolly difficult to drag that victim along grass. Impossible, in fact, without subjecting oneself to capture. It was agreed between the two teams that there would be a truce during the running of the race. When the first runners returned to school, or at three-fifteen (whichever is the sooner), the contest would be on again until three thirty-five. This would also give us the chance to support Normal Nesbitt in action.

(M. de B.)

Alsopp: *Memo to Self*

Thank goodness for the Halliwell Bowl. There has been a distinct dip in ankle-grabbing now that the race is being run. My theory is that people need something big and important to focus their attention on and the race has provided it. There has never been such interest in the event before. This concentration on discipline and stamina is tremendously important, I feel, and it's come along at just the right time. I suspect that things will pretty much revert to normal when the race is over.

Nesbitt: **The Two Nesbitts**

I stopped running and looked back down the avenue which I expected to be empty now. It wasn't. The Hunk was cycling towards me. He was shouting and from the look on his face he'd been shouting for some time.

"Nesbitt, Nesbitt. What the hell do you think you're playing at?"

Three or four other runners were trudging up the avenue behind him like chicks following a mother hen. He was about to yell at me again, but he must've heard them coming because he suddenly went rigid trying to grip the brakes. The bike slewed to a stop with a squeal.

"Get back, you clowns," he cried over his shoulder. "It's not down here!"

They stopped running and looked puzzled as he jumped from his bike and began sprinting towards them.

"Turn off! Turn off!"

"Pardon, sir?" one of them shouted.

"It's not straight on. You have to turn off at the crossroads. Go on! Get moving. Left, left, left!"

They looked at each other, completely bemused for a second or two. Then one of them trundled off back down the avenue and the others fell in behind him. They reached the crossroads and turned left.

"No!" screamed Holloway. "You berks! Left, left, left! Your left, not mine!"

By then, though, he was chasing down the avenue after them and their left *was* his.

I didn't wait for them to sort it all out; I carried on running straight, away from them and the Halliwell Bowl and Claire and everything. I didn't know where I was heading and I didn't much care. The thoughts I'd been keeping out of my head all that time came rushing in like a wind. I had the strange sensation that I was running alongside myself and that the two Nesbitts were in the middle of an argument:

What a stupid, gutless thing to do.

Why? Why was it gutless?

Because you were doing so well.

It doesn't matter any more. Nothing matters.

154

OK. Then you're stuck with it. Normal Nesbitt. That's what you are and that's what you'll remain now.

There are more important things than the Halliwell Bowl.

You weren't running for the Halliwell Bowl. You were running for yourself. Isn't that important?

I'm not bothered.

Then why are you still running now?

No reason. It doesn't matter. I'll stop if it bothers you. Right? Satisfied? We're walking now.

So nothing matters, does it?

Not much.

What about people? Friends?

You must be joking.

Brains is a friend. Or he was till you chilled him out.

Brains is a fool. What about that girl in Clacton? He wrote about four hundred letters to that girl and never got one answer. He pretends it was a big romance. He's a fool.

So what about Claire?

She can get lost.

You're obsessed with the girl, you know.

Rubbish.

You are. She stands for everything you're not.

Piss off.

She's talented and clever and beautiful and you're dull and ordinary and average.

I said, piss off!

And normal. Absolutely Normal Nesbitt!

I broke into a run again, trying to get away. I came to the end of the avenue and found three streets of large houses ahead of me. Hoping that the other Nesbitt would take the street on the left, I headed down the one on the right.

Brains: *The House of Cards*

Word came back down the line like a lit fuse. Nesbitt's done a bunk. He's run out of the race. I didn't believe it, even with all the other wobbly things going on all over the place. I thought maybe he was so far ahead by now that people were just getting confused. But it was true. He had done a bunk.

The effect on the others was amazing. It was like Nesbitt was the one cog that kept all the machinery of the race going. Once he'd packed up, everything came to a standstill. Everything except Holloway, who was not best pleased.

He gave chase for a bit, but that meant the following group was left without a check-point so they didn't know where to go. They ran after Holloway, ran back again, ran left, ran right. Eventually they stopped and formed a ragged group which wasn't going anywhere. And Holloway leapt off his bike, bellowing and having kittens all over the road.

Then someone from the group saw Nesbitt in the distance. Apparently he was leaning against a tree and watching all this going on. They all thought, what is this? Has Nesbitt dipped out, or what? And guessed that he had. At first it puzzled them and they stood around for a while, not quite knowing what to do. The longer they stood there, of course, the bigger the group got because other runners were turning up all the time. Maybe, if someone had been decisive and carried on running straight away, the race might have continued. But no one was being decisive – at least, no one but Nesbitt – and the impetus had gone, and they began to think, "Oh, what the hell", and some of them decided they'd drop out too. It sort of spread outwards from there and within minutes people were dropping out like flies. A few runners from the other schools stuck to the course for a while in a half-hearted way, but eventually they began to surrender to the Nesbitt effect too.

Some people went for their own gentle jog, though not many of them stuck to the course. Some even went back the way they'd come. Others simply stopped and rested or wandered off home. It played hell with the traffic. Apparently one or two cars swerved to avoid ambling runners and a few tailbacks began to build up. There were even reports of fighting breaking out between motorists, although I saw nothing of it.

In a very short time my check-point had turned into a kind of picnic area. People were stretched out on the ground eating sandwiches. Don't ask me where they'd got them from – it was the sort of day when sandwiches could just appear. I must say, it was all very weird, but the atmosphere was certainly relaxed. I mean, it was a mutiny really, I suppose, but it didn't look like one.

The whole bloody house of cards has caved in, I thought. Not just the race, but the school and all it stands for. I felt a moment of panic and then it passed. I thought, it's a nice day. Let's enjoy ourselves.

I was chatting to a group of lads from St Peter's when Jackie Maugham came sprinting up. She stood out from the crowd a bit because, by this time, she was the only person running. She grabbed my elbow and pulled me aside.

"Hey!" I said. "What's going on?"

"I found the body," she said.

"You what?"

"What you saw in the gym. With Gordon. I've found the body."

I swear that all the birds stopped singing at that moment and not a sound could be heard. I couldn't believe it. A body. Not just beating someone up but... My God. I couldn't even bring myself to say the word.

So why was Jackie still grinning? She'd cracked. Poor kid. It was too much for her and she'd gone completely to pieces. She'd found the body and come running straight to me. More than half a mile.

"It was the dummy," she said, still grinning.

"Calm down, Jackie," I said, taking her by the shoulders. "It's OK now. Everything's going to be OK."

Once again I felt like the only sane person on the planet and I wasn't quite sure what to do about it.

"Listen to me, Brains," she went on. "It wasn't a kid at all. No blood, no injuries. It was a stuffed dummy. Noddy was beating up Miss Cassidy's dummy."

Alsopp: *Memo to Self*

Settled down to a mound of paperwork, piled up over the weeks, when there was a phone call from the police. (Trying to keep calm about this as I write, but it's not easy.)

Was I aware that there was a race going on in town?

"Yes," I said. "We let you know about it. You should check your records."

"We did know about it," said the policeman on the phone. "What we didn't know about was the picnics."

"Picnics?"

"Yes, sir. The picnics in the middle of the road. Blocking the traffic."

"Oh, dear..."

"And the runners walking arm in arm against the flow and trotting off in all directions across the flow. Blocking more traffic. We didn't know you were going to bring the whole bleeding town to a grinding bloody halt. Sir."

"Oh, dear..."

"Indeed, sir. Bit of a cock-up, wouldn't you say so, sir? Any suggestions?"

I didn't have much choice. I grovelled for a second or two, then slammed the phone down and made for the car park. Things had gone too far. Stop being nice, Alsopp, I told myself. Stop trying to understand. Get out on that cross country course and start knocking heads together.

Who is doing this to me? That's what I want to know. Who wants to bring me down like this?

159

My road led to a footbridge over the railway line and then, quite by chance, to the town centre. I'd never been that way before so I wasn't expecting to end up in town. I trotted up an alley way and suddenly I was in the middle of the High Street. For a few more seconds I carried on jogging into the thick of people. There wasn't much of a choice, really. The only alternative was to turn round and head back for the avenue and I couldn't face that. There was no point in running any more, though. In fact I felt a bit of a prat – a runner, complete with cardboard number, but no sign of a race to run in. I ripped the number off the front of my T-shirt and stuffed it in a bin.

Cool down, Gordon, I told myself. Look as if you're supposed to be here. Wander, look in shop windows, take your time. The trouble was, my head was still running and I couldn't focus properly on where I was. I loitered around a shop window for a while and tried to look nonchalant. Then I noticed that it was Mothercare and I hurried on to the next shop. That was better – a baker's. I could buy a sausage roll or something; look a bit more purposeful. Except, of course, that I had no money.

As I turned away from the baker's I caught sight of my reflection. I still had a carboard number flapping about on my back. An old man with a shopping trolley stopped beside me. He was one of those sorts who wear two cardigans and a tweed jacket whatever the weather. He gave me a sidelong

160

glance and I smiled at him, angling my back away. Not that there was much point. If the old man didn't see that I had a number on my back then someone else would. The only way I could prevent that was to lean against a wall. Or take my T-shirt off and unpin the number.

The old boy edged his trolley off without returning my smile. It's now or never, I thought, and started to pull the T-shirt over my head.

When you think about how the universe works, I mean how it actually ticks over, planets and stars all whizzing through space in some kind of relationship with each other, it's incredible how things turn out sometimes. Things like Jeanette coming out of the baker's at the very moment that my head was about to emerge from the T-shirt. Maybe it wouldn't be so strange for *someone* to come out of the baker's at that moment. The town was pretty crowded. People were going in and out of shops all the time. But *Jeanette*? At that very moment? The most sarcastic, inquisitive person I knew. A member of my family. It could only be that there was some kind of Guiding Force in the Great Beyond who decided to stretch down a finger and poke me in the eye.

I looked through the tunnel of my T-shirt, saw a pasty white face beneath a circle of jet black hair that I *knew* was Jeanette and I froze. If I had to choose one person to let the whole world know where I was and what I was doing, that person would be Jeanette. She had an incredible talent for drawing attention to herself and anyone else she happened to be with. She would, in the first place, screech and make everyone in the centre of town turn and look. Then she would question me in a loud voice.

"You're in a race, Gordon? What do you mean you're in a race? *What* race? I see no race. And *why* are you in a race?"

(By this time shoppers would be hurrying from all corners of town and thronging round to see what was going on.)

"Because you're normal, Gordon? You're behaving like this because you're normal?"

(And now traffic would be grinding to a standstill, drivers craning out of windows. In fact, it seemed as if the traffic *was* seizing up. There was a hell of a lot of hooting going on – *PARP-parp*, *PARP-parp*. *NES-bitt*, *NES-bitt*.)

And she'd *force* me to mention Claire.

"Claire Brooks? Speak up, Gordon. You mean that blonde piece from school?"

"That's right," the crowd would shout. "We knew there was a girl involved. He's been staring at the window of Mothercare!"

And everyone would know, everyone would be looking at me. And Mum would turn up. Jeanette would see that Mum would turn up out of the blue.

"Gordon, what are you doing, stripping off in front of all these people? What's the matter with you? Don't you care what people think of us?"

There would be no point in my saying anything. Mum would know what was wrong at a glance. It could only be one thing. Acute constipation.

"Ladies and gentlemen, the boy is clearly constipated. Take pity on him. Someone send for an ambulance! He needs instant treatment. He should be given an injection of prune juice and locked in a darkened bathroom till he's sorted himself out!"

All this stretched before me as I stared at my sister down the tunnel of my half-removed T-shirt. Jeanette turned towards me, frowned and looked away again. Thank God! She didn't recognize me. I didn't give her a second chance and scuttled off at a crouch with my head still inside the T-shirt. I overtook the old man with the shopping trolley. He swerved out of my way and took refuge in a bus shelter. It must've been a bit disturbing for him, out for a little quiet shopping only to find himself pursued by a headless dwarf with a number on his back.

When I was sure that I'd lost Jeanette, I whipped the T-shirt off and tugged at the number. It came away with a rip. Still, it was better to be wearing a shirt with a hole in than a cardboard number. My heart was pounding and I was red in the face so I sat down on a bench to rest.

I looked at the shopping crowds as they threaded their way all around me. Then, from their midst, I saw another face I knew. Someone walking towards my bench. Walking easily, looking from side to side. It reminded me of a day in the park some weeks ago. Brains nudging my leg and saying, "Look who's coming." And a blonde girl walking out of the wood into the sunlight. Looking from side to side as she was now.

Brains: *A Friend in Need*

So Noddy had duffed up a dummy and not a kid from the lower school. It was a big relief to learn this. It was also fairly painful. I could see from the pitying look in Jackie's eyes that she thought I was a fart of very little brain, not even worth the taking of a novelty photo. Also, of course, there was Noddy himself. The last time I'd seen him I'd run alongside and hurled abuse at him. And, at that stage, he was probably thinking I was his only friend. It's all very well having a fan club in your honour, but that doesn't mean you have friends, does it? Not real friends.

So where was he now, I thought? And what sort of misery was he going through? I felt I should go and look for him, offer some words of comfort and a helping hand. Maybe even say sorry.

But that was not to be. For one thing I had no idea where he was. For another the peace was shaken by the vicious slamming of a car door. I spun round and Madge Alsopp was steaming into view, and not looking as if he was in the mood for an exchange of pleasantries.

Nesbitt: The Last Domino

I sat for some moments looking at her, feeling that it was both very strange and perfectly natural to see her here, in town at this time. It didn't seem wrong and it didn't strike me as odd that I'd been running behind her down an avenue of trees earlier in the afternoon. That she shouldn't have been here, in fact. She wore not running gear but jeans and a white blouse. It shouldn't have been possible. I sat and watched her as she came nearer and nearer. Should I move? Hide? I didn't know, but in any case I didn't feel like any more running. I watched her until she was almost level with me. Then she looked towards my bench and saw me. Her look didn't pass through me this time. She noticed me and stopped in her tracks.

"Nesbitt?" she said. "What are you doing here?"

And that, believe it or not, was the first time she'd spoken to me without someone else, like Brains mostly, hovering around. Actually we were far from alone – the town was busy with shoppers. No one was paying us any attention, though, and it felt – I don't know – as if we were in the middle of an empty field or something. She sat down beside me on the bench, looking anxiously around, as if she was afraid that we would be spotted.

"What are you doing here?" she asked again.

"I was in the race. Just behind you. Holloway was at the check-point."

"You were? You mean, actually in the race?"

"Yes. I just said I was."

She didn't even know I'd been running. I started to feel the old anger coming back. She was so absorbed in herself and what she could do that she didn't even know I was in it, in spite of the fact that the whole school had been talking about it. Vast sums of money were changing hands because I was in it. And she didn't even know.

"You're not making sense, Gordon," she said, standing up and backing away a little with timid steps. "If you were in the race what are you doing here?"

"Never mind what I'm doing here," I said. "I *was* in the race. I even got past Metson and you were just in front of me when we were running down the avenue. You were wearing a blue vest."

"No," she said with a little shake of her head. "That wasn't me. You made a mistake..."

"Didn't you wear a blue vest?"

"I'm telling you. No. It wasn't me. I dropped out. I didn't even start."

Dropped out? So who had I been following up the avenue? It was a blonde in a blue vest. Same length of hair. Running well, running easily. But I hadn't seen her face and I'd jumped to conclusions. She hadn't noticed that I was in the race and I hadn't noticed that she wasn't.

When I looked round at Claire she had stood up and was going. She was already partly obscured by all the people milling about between us.

"Wait!" I shouted, jumping up. "You can't just go like that."

She must've heard me because she quickened her step. I ran after her but a man with a briefcase got in my way. We did a little dance together, each side-stepping in the same direction and muttering sorry. The man stopped and laughed but I was in no mood to be polite and I pushed by him. By the time I got free, Claire was almost out of sight. I skipped and swerved through the crowd until I caught up with her.

"What do you mean, you weren't in the race?" I asked.

"I don't mean anything. I just didn't run, that's all. It's nothing to do with you."

"It is. Of course it is." I back-pedalled, trying to look her in the eye, but she kept turning her head to avoid me. "I only entered the bloody thing because you were in it."

"What?" she said, stopping abruptly.

"I said I entered because you were in it."

"But why? That's stupid."

"No, it isn't. It's perfectly normal. You know me. Normal Nesbitt. I don't do stupid things."

"Well, you can't blame me because you entered. It was your decision."

And she darted off again.

"I'm not blaming you," I called. "I just want to know why you didn't run."

"It's nothing to do with you. Leave me alone."

This was wonderful. The first chance to talk to her and it had developed into a public slanging match. She was weaving in and out of the crowds and I kept nipping ahead and running backwards, trying to look her in the eye.

But maybe that's what I wanted. A row. I once thought it was. To tell her what I thought; quite straight. The trouble was that now I was doing it I felt all wrong.

"Leave you alone?" I said. "It's a bit late for that, isn't it? Didn't you do that article?"

"Article?"

I grabbed her arms to stop her moving away and she flinched. I was expecting her to struggle, but the way she flinched took me by surprise. She seemed to fold up so that, instead of preventing her from getting away, I was supporting her. She shook her head and her hair spun round, like the tail of a horse, flicking me lightly across the face.

"Please," she said. "I don't want to talk about it."

That's what she said, but she looked as if she meant the opposite. Her face said, "I do want to talk about it. Please." I had to get her out of the crowd and find somewhere quiet. I looked round. Nothing but faces and shoulders and bulging shopping bags. And someone pushing through the crowd with a bike.

"Nesbitt! Stay exactly where you are!"

Holloway's face was shining with sweat and rage. His front wheel cut a way through the press of bodies, and he stood stock still, fixing me with his eyes.

"I want a word with you, Nesbitt," he said.

He said "word" as if he meant "punch-up". He was about to add something else when he noticed Claire, stopped and pushed his head towards us, as if he couldn't quite believe what he was seeing.

"What the hell's going on here?" he said, hardly moving his mouth. The words seemed to come out of his nostrils, quiet but perfectly audible in spite of the crowd. In fact the only other sound I was aware of was not the bustle of shoppers but the click of his bike edging forward. Neither Claire nor I spoke.

"It's chaos back there, Nesbitt," Holloway said.

I looked vaguely over his shoulder at the throng of shoppers.

"Not there," he snapped. "Back at the race. Back at what used to be the race."

"Used to be?"

"It's not a race any more. It's sheer bloody mayhem. You're responsible and I..." He took another step nearer. "I am going to find out why."

I found myself holding on to his handlebars, trying to keep the bike between us, bracing myself for an attack. He thrust the bike at me with a sudden movement and I jumped, lifting my knee in a reflex action. The brake block dug into my leg, but for half a minute I felt no pain.

"Hold on to my bike for a moment," he said, turning away from me. "Are you all right, Claire?"

She didn't answer.

"I think I ought to get you home, don't you?"

Which would've been the perfect end to the perfect day. Talking to Claire – all right then, arguing with Claire, but at least *with* her – when Hunk Holloway gallops in on his charger to rescue her from a dangerous loony in a ripped T-shirt. But Claire looked quickly at his face and then darted off into the crowd. For a fraction of a second Holloway and I stared at each other, united in puzzlement. Then, without thinking, I pushed him in the chest, saw him totter back, and ran off in the opposite direction.

"You sod, Nesbitt!"

Run, run, Gordon. For God's sake why can't you run quicker? I couldn't understand why I was going so slowly until I realized my hands were still gripping the handlebars of Holloway's bike. So I swung into the saddle as I ran, kicked at the spinning pedals and bumped down the kerb into the road.

Brains: *A Sweet Discovery in a Moment of Crisis*

"You are not simply a disgrace to your schools," Alsopp was saying, "you are a disgrace to the youth of this country. Look at yourselves."

The runners were standing in a huddle with their heads bowed. They didn't bother to look at themselves – they knew what he meant. He took a pace or two towards them and their eyes dropped even further. They were now looking at the ground between their feet. He paused in front of the shiny green vest of a bloke I'd never seen before. A tall bloke. Alsopp was practically staring up his nostrils.

"What have you got behind your back?" asked Alsopp in an uncanny, sweet voice.

The bloke in the green vest said nothing, but slowly extended his hand with half a pork pie on it. The Head gazed on it with contempt.

"You utter, utter wimp," he said. "We are about to walk back to the school and that will be dropped in the first bin we pass."

This was not the man who was smiling nicely at me from behind his comfortable desk the other day. This was a man in a corner, fighting his way out. The birds in the trees huddled together for protection and old ladies dragged fluffy dogs quickly by in case he should snatch one up and bite its head off.

Jackie and I watched the runners as they began to troop back to school in a silent line, two abreast. Now that would've made a good photograph. I glanced at Jackie, but I could see she was keeping her camera well out of the way. Thank goodness. One twitch and it would've gone the way of the pork pie. Not much time to feel too relieved, though. Madge's march past drew level with us and he skewered me with a look that sent shivers into my soul.

"Baines," he hissed. "What are you doing here?"

"I'm a marshal, sir."

"Right. I shall want a full report on this afternoon's events. A full report."

And his voice was full of blame. Something is seriously amiss here, Baines. Someone is to blame and I have strong suspicions that it must be you.

I swallowed. Jackie squeezed my arm. She gave me a nervous smile and I noticed something about her which had escaped my attention until that moment.

She had dark hair and blue eyes.

Nesbitt: On the Run

Holloway must've been torn between running after Claire to throw a protective arm round her shoulders, and running after me to twist my head off. What was uppermost in his mind? Helping her or murdering me? Whatever it was, the hesitation gave me just enough time to get clear.

I veered round a parked van and almost skinned the side of a bus. Someone yelled some obscene advice at my back. However, two turnings down side streets with crowds closing behind me like the Red Sea and I was well clear of Holloway. I was free, for the moment, but I was also riding a stolen vehicle so I got off and left it propped against a wall.

I walked down to the river, to the point where it bends into town, and leaned against the bridge, just looking into the water. And waiting. What for? I don't know. It just felt like waiting. I don't know how long I stayed there either. I lost all notion of time and place. I almost forgot where I was and didn't notice the thinning of the crowds.

Well, I thought. You've made a pig's ear out of all this and no mistake. Desertion, attacking a teacher and stealing his bike. To say nothing of shouting at Claire. Well done, Gordon. Well done. You're going to have a busy time explaining your way out of this one.

And what about Claire? What was the matter with her? Running away from Holloway. Being in town in the first place. And saying she hadn't been in the race. What was that about?

No amount of staring at the river below could answer those questions for me and I began to assume I'd never find out. I was wrong about that, though. I heard someone say my name and I looked up from the river to see her standing a little way off.

"I've been looking for you for ages," she said. "Can we go somewhere to talk?"

Alsopp: *Memo to Self*

I was right. I was damn well right. One person *was* at the bottom of it all. The influence of one person has made the entire establishment totter. And who was that one person? Gordon Nesbitt.

So, of course, in a way I was wrong as well. I thought I'd sorted Nesbitt out. I even thought at one stage that he was the only normal person around the place. Very, very wrong, Alsopp. What happened to your basic psychological training? Where were your powers of observation when you needed them? Gordon Nesbitt normal? Nesbitt is not, never was and probably never will be normal.

What caused those outbreaks of violence in the Lower School? Nesbitt. He's the cult figure behind this freakish behaviour. I was blind not to see it.

Who has wasted hour after hour of precious administrative time? Nesbitt. I thought I was lending a hand to a kid in trouble. I'm now pretty damn sure he was stringing me along.

Who brought the shame of the Halliwell Bowl fiasco tumbling round our ears? Nesbitt. This was the missing piece that completed the jigsaw. Nesbitt led a mutiny of over a hundred athletes on the public highway. I find myself shaking now at the thought of it.

Who caused the town to grind to, as the police so aptly put it, a bleeding halt? Nesbitt. Nesbitt, Nesbitt, Nesbitt. Every time.

Just look at the effect he's had on my staff. Holloway was a gibbering wreck when I found him out on the course. He told me Nesbitt was to blame and then he went storming off on his bike, absolutely bent on revenge. I didn't blame him, but some of the things he was spouting were, to say the least, unprofessional. Cassidy and Peck have become obsessed by Nesbitt. Peck jibbers of nothing but Nesbitt – he's more or less abandoned all duties to run computer programs on the little sod – and Cassidy wants to mount a ridiculous vaudeville act entirely constructed around him.

Never before have I had to think so quickly or take such drastic action. It's played the bloody monkey with my digestive system and has done, I now realize, for the past few weeks. I've called a general assembly. I'm going to address the school. Re-establish authority. Time for the iron fist in the iron glove!

Minutes of a Second Emergency Meeting of the Normal Nesbitt Fan Club

Or, to be exact, a meeting of half of the original committee. Members present: M. de Beere and F. Whale. Things are getting desperate. J. Corduroy and S. James are 10 points clear and there are only minutes left before the Normal Nesbitt competition is due to close. The school is in a state of panic. It's hard to tell what's been going on out there, but runners are coming back all the time with teachers snapping at their heels. Of course, whatever it is, Normal Nesbitt must be behind it. This is good, but we can't find out what it's all about just yet. We must move quickly if we are to win the day. And the Normal Nesbitt Fan Club was my idea so it's only right that I should end up on top. F. Whale is not so keen on my plan, but he will do what I say, especially if we wear Balaclava helmets. We need more than ten points. We need to put the competition out of the reach of the others. We need the Big One. All systems go.

(M. de B.)

Brains: *The Last Straw*

There was still no news of Noddy when we got back to school. All the other runners had been found and hauled in, but there were funny rumours going round about the phantom Nesbitt. Toby told me that Alsopp himself had discovered Noddy in town somewhere. He was about to haul him back when Noddy took a plunge into the crowd and was off again. But you know what rumours are like. It was a nice thought, but somehow it didn't ring true. Gordon Nesbitt attacking our noble Head? I think not. Unless, of course, he'd popped right out of his trolley as a result of recent events. And recent events included me calling him a vicious bastard. In fact that could've been the last straw. A pretty uncomfortable thought.

"What are we going to do?" I asked Jackie.

She shrugged. There was nothing we could do until Noddy showed up and even then I was doubtful that he could be set back on the right tracks so easily. The problem was that Noddy had spent all his life being ordinary and predictable. Now he'd flipped, everything could be very different. The worst sinner is the converted saint. He could've been in town at that very moment – pillaging, smashing things up, rioting.

"He can't riot by himself," said Jackie.

But I wasn't so sure. I could imagine the damage – boxes of apples and stuff being kicked all over the place; old biddies with shopping trolleys fleeing into public conveniences for safety. And Gordon Nesbitt with his teeth bared, laughing like a drain.

Nesbitt: A Date With Claire

Leaving the bridge we walked silently back towards the town centre till we came across a burger bar. We found one of those window seats where you have to crouch like a Cossack before you can slide yourself in. Not the best kind of seat in those circumstances – I felt trapped and it was difficult to avoid looking straight at Claire. She wanted to talk, she said, but neither of us was saying anything.

In the end I had to speak because the waitress sidled over and stood between us, chewing and waiting for an order.

"Oh," I said, looking at Claire as casually as I could. "Would you like something to drink?"

"Yes. Thanks."

"Coffee or something?"

"Coffee. Fine."

"Or a milkshake? I mean they're not good for you and they're a bit sludgy, but if you'd rather…"

"Coffee, Gordon," she said shortly. "Coffee will be fine."

"Right," I said to the waitress. "Coffee, please. And er…"

Maybe I should order something to eat, I thought. The mood didn't seem right for burger and chips, though, and as soon as I thought of food I remembered that I had no money. In fact I'd offered Claire a coffee and I couldn't pay for it. Oh, sod it, I thought. I'll cross that bridge when we come to it.

The waitress slid off with a sniff and there it was again – the silence. The world turned on its axis some more; I stifled a sigh; Claire studied the table top. Then she said,

"What article?"

"Pardon?"

"You said I did an article or something."

"Well, yes. You did. About me being average."

"Oh, that."

"Yes, that."

"It didn't mean anything. No one took it seriously, did they?"

"I did."

"Then you shouldn't be so sensitive. You weren't meant to take it seriously. Not that seriously, anyway."

"Oh, I'm sorry," I said querulously. "I didn't realize. I hope I didn't spoil the joke."

"But that's all it was, Gordon. A joke."

"Yes, but it also happened to be true. And that's what hurt…"

"True? How can a joke be true?"

"I *was* average. Still am. Completely average. A freak. I didn't know it till you were kind enough to point it out. And nor did anyone else, either."

"Of course you're not average. No one is that average. It's just not possible..."

"Look, I've been through all this a hundred times already. I am average. Ask Alsopp if you don't believe me. I'm so bloody normal that I hardly exist. I fade into the background most of the time."

She looked at me, frowning slightly as if I were some kind of mathematical problem on a page. Nesbitt the Statistic. A few seconds working him out and then you can forget about him. The waitress brought the coffee, set it down and hovered.

"Anything else?"

"No," I said. "Thank you."

"You can't just have one coffee. It's after two o'clock. You have to have items to the value of two fifty."

"Do we?"

"Yes," she said, folding her arms. "Or you can't have the coffee."

I thought about walking out, but I'd had enough of that for one day – the race, the confrontation with Holloway and now a burger bar. You had to draw the line somewhere and face up to things.

"All right, then," I said. "If that's the way it is. Burger and chips. OK?"

"OK," she said and shuffled off.

"Without onion," I called, but either she didn't hear or she was deliberately ignoring me.

"Look," I said when she'd gone, "tell me about the race. I don't understand why you weren't in it."

"I told you. I didn't start."

"But why? Are you all right?"

"I'm not injured, if that's what you mean. I just didn't want to run."

"You dropped out?"

"Yes."

"Claire," I said, tapping the table in exasperation. "This is ridiculous. You could've won. You would've won. I know you would."

"Does that matter?"

"What do you mean, does it matter? You're the one who spent every available minute training. You had Brains out there going into spasms with that stop-watch hour after hour. What was all that about if you didn't want to win?"

She didn't answer immediately, but looked down at her untouched coffee and fiddled with a plastic spoon in her fingers.

"I can't explain it properly. I just got tired of living up to expectations."

Then the waitress was with us again. How can you talk about these things with food and drink whizzing about all over the place? It seemed so ridiculous.

"One burger and chips with," the waitress said sharply.

"With?" I asked. "With what?"

"With onion. Will that be all?"

"How much does it come to?"

"Two fifty-five."

"Then that's all."

She ripped a sheet off her note pad, slapped it on the table and stalked off.

"I suddenly felt that that was all I was doing," said Claire, as if there hadn't been any interruption. "Living up to expectations."

"I don't get it," I said. "What expectations?"

"The race for a start. Brains expected me to win, Holloway expected me to win. Almost everyone did in the end."

"I still don't see..."

"I could cope with that if that was all. But there's work..."

"Work? Your work is brilliant. What's the matter with that?"

"I'm supposed to succeed all the time. Top of this, top of that. Exams. Pass, pass, pass. On to University. Ticking off the achievements as I go..."

"Sounds OK to me," I said.

"Well it's not OK, Gordon. I'm a person, not just a box of clever tricks. And people aren't treating me as if I'm a person. They treat me as if I'm perfect or something."

"And that worries you? You want to try being average."

"I don't want to try being anything. I don't want to be ... measured up any more. That's why I didn't turn up for the race. I'd had enough of being labelled."

"What?" I said. "You? I'm the one who's labelled. I'm nothing but label."

"Really?" And she looked at me hard for a second. "The Dumb Blonde? Isn't that a label?"

Oh, God. That.

I imagined myself saying the name – to Brains, to Metson, even to Colin. I saw my stupid face forming the words.

"We didn't mean..." I mumbled.

"We?" she said.

"I mean me. I didn't..."

"No, of course you didn't."

"Look, I'm sorry."

Then she sighed and looked at me in a way I'll never forget. A full blast of a look: disdain and pity; regret and something else, something I couldn't work out at all.

"No," she said. "It was stupid, but I can live with it. What I did was worse."

"What you did? What did you do?"

"The article. That was deliberate. I calculated that."

"Deliberate? But... but..."

"I could've picked on any one of them. I don't know why I chose you. That averages thing came up, I suppose, and I just went ahead."

"You did it on purpose?"

"You wouldn't talk to me, Gordon. I was like a doll to you lot. So I wanted to show you. I wanted to get back at you. But it got out of hand," she said. "And I'm sorry."

She was sorry.

Brains: *The Crackdown*

We soon learnt how serious things had become. Madge had called a general assembly, everyone to be in the main hall immediately. This was it – the crackdown.

The corridors were buzzing with speculation, but as we filed nearer to the hall a deadly silence fell over us. Alsopp was standing by the double doors and looking white-faced and grim. No more sweet smiles and words of wisdom. The régime of understanding was obviously over and we were in for the backlash. "Hand Nesbitt over or twenty of your people will be taken outside and thrashed."

We were only a dozen paces from Alsopp when I noticed a tiny movement at floor level behind him. Two slight figures on hands and knees, their faces obscured by Balaclavas. Jackie noticed them too and nudged me.

"What are they up to?"

The figures crawled closer. Suddenly I knew what they were up to and a chill ran through me.

"They can't," I said. "They can't possibly. Not Alsopp. Not now..."

But they could. And they did.

I must admit they made a pretty neat job of it. They'd picked the worst possible moment, but you had to admire the way they brought it off. There was a severe look on Alsopp's face as he stood there watching people into the Hall. His arms were folded and his brows creased in a frown.

"Don't talk out of the side of your mouth, Keeble," he was saying, "otherwise you'll... *Whoaaghh!*"

And down he went. His mouth was open like a large round cave and his arms flung upwards, as if he was finishing a big number in an American musical.

They only pulled him about a yard or two. Then they let go of his ankles and bolted like rabbits with their heads well down. One flew up the corridor and the other down. It was a very professional piece of work and they deserved all the points they must've got for it. But, oh dear, it was a bad day to choose.

The file of people heading for the Hall stopped and fell back. A respectful circle formed round the motionless Madge and people were beginning to wonder what to do, when his fingers began to flex. Then he tried to collect himself and stand with some dignity. His face was twisted as he turned to us.

He made a wailing sound like a cross between a wolf and a steam whistle.

"Someone is going to pay for this!" he yelled.

I knew exactly what he meant by someone.

Nesbitt: Muscling In

We'd divided the burger into equal pieces. I'd eaten mine some time ago, but Claire's was untouched. There were yellow and white fragments of chips, like polystyrene crumbs, over half the table and the waitress kept glaring at us from behind the counter. I don't know why. There were other seats around. Maybe she thought we were putting people off by sitting near the window. Not that I cared.

We were talking. Not about anything important.

Colin. Running. Brains. I can't remember it all. Just chat. And I was able to look at her without flinching or going red. I was looking at her when I noticed her stiffen, and in the same moment a large body swung quickly into the seat next to me, blocking my way out. I turned slowly and found myself staring into the flared nostrils of Holloway.

"Oh, hello, sir," I said. "Did you manage to get your bike back, then?"

"Nesbitt," he said in a low voice that might've sounded friendly if you didn't know, "don't speak to me. Don't say a word. I've just been through the most humiliating afternoon of my whole life because of you, and the mere sound of your voice might just be enough to make me do something I might regret in years to come."

"He hasn't done anything, Mr Holloway," said Claire.

He riveted his attention on the torn-up chips and lowered his voice even further.

"Hasn't done anything? Hasn't done anything? My dear girl, I can't begin to tell you what he's done."

We struggled to the door with Holloway holding my arm so firmly that I felt as if the rest of my body was dangling from the shoulder. A bit like raw meat hanging from a butcher's hook.

"Excuse me."

It was the waitress, shuffling over at speed. Holloway attempted to wave her away.

"It's all right," he said. "They're with me."

"Well you can pay, then. Two fifty-five. Service not included."

Holloway darted a violent look at me and dug into his pockets.

Claire looked at me and smiled.

Minutes of the Final Meeting of the Normal Nesbitt Fan Club

Four members present. A brief discussion about the winning of the last Normal Nesbitt competition. Some members thought that the winning team had shown true courage and resourcefulness. Others said that it was dangerous and because of it the club had lost most of its membership.

A sad moment came when the club was disbanded. It was thought that we could carry on, but it didn't really make sense to have a Normal Nesbitt Fan Club without Normal Nesbitt.

It was agreed to hold a meeting soon to discuss a change of activities.

(M. de B.)

Alsopp: *Memo to Self*

I've just passed on the Nesbitt files – three boxes of stuff I'd collected myself, plus the psychologist's report and statements from Holloway and Cassidy. Peck was all for sending a bloody great pile of computer print-outs he'd run off, but I talked him out of it.

So, at long last we're free of him. I saw him one last time, as I had to, to explain the procedures for his going. He's a cool customer. Seeing him standing there in my room with his hands behind his back, you'd never believe he was capable of all that destruction. I told him what would be happening and he just nodded and looked a little crestfallen, as if butter wouldn't melt in his mouth.

He had to go. There was no alternative and I'm not going to feel bad about it. Anyone else would have done the same in my position. I had the good of the school to consider. Anyway, he's got the chance of a fresh start in a new school. And I didn't involve the police when I might easily have done so. He's lucky, really. Starting again with a clean sheet. Best thing all round.

Brains: *The Art of Photography*

I wish I'd found out about cameras and things a lot sooner because I think it's something I have a real knack for.

The great thing about photography is that it's art. You make beautiful images. If you could see this portrait I've done of Jackie you'd know exactly what I mean. And I'm talking about a proper portrait here. Nothing smutty. I wouldn't consider anything that wasn't tasteful, believe me. Not any more. I'm a changed man. She's sort of looking off to one side, as if she's seeing something in the distance, and it really is fantastic. Dark hair, blue eyes, faraway look. Wonderful.

Also it actually triggers the past in your head.

Photography, I mean. You think you remember things pretty clearly, but you don't. There's a ton of stuff you just don't remember at all. Only when you see a photograph does your memory start working properly. That's how it happened with me.

I'd gone round to Jackie's house and she was showing me some of her pictures. She's had them put on card and they look really nice. Funny too, some of them. We were having a laugh at a few she took of Metson making a pilchard of himself on the school field. There was one of him doing this knees-up routine that was classic. Puffed-out cheeks, bulging eyes, the lot. They weren't all funny, though. One of them showed his trainers in a pile. You wouldn't think trainers could be interesting, but these were.

"It's the composition," she explained. "The way you see it in the viewfinder."

Then she flipped over the trainers and there was this face staring out at us. Mouth open, a bit startled. Leaning against the brick pillar at the school gate. And we went quiet for a moment.

"Gordon," said Jackie.

"Yes," I said. "Gordon."

Well, we both knew it was Gordon. Of course. There wasn't much else we could say about it, though. He'd been gone for about a month, I suppose. I won't say I'd forgotten about him – you don't forget people like Gordon Nesbitt – but I hadn't thought about him for a while. And I hadn't seen him since he'd been expelled.

Well, that's not quite true. I did see him once. He

187

was out walking his dog, Colin, and I was the other side of the river. I almost called out to him.

"Oi, Noddy! How goes it?"

But he hadn't seen me and something kept my mouth shut. I don't know what. Maybe I felt bad about him going like that. Maybe I just didn't know what we'd have to talk about any more.

"I wonder how he is," said Jackie.

"Yes, I wonder."

"We ought to go and see, perhaps."

"Yes," I said. "Why not?"

And I thought I would. Just pop in to see how he was, have a bit of a chat. It didn't occur to me till I saw his face gawping up at me from Jackie's photo: I missed him. The place was, I don't know, dull without him.

Nesbitt: Starting From Scratch

The good weather came to an end. I was walking by the river with Colin. You could feel cool drizzle on your face but it wasn't hard enough to mark the surface of the water. I ambled along, flicking bits of twig into the river and Colin followed at the end of a slack lead. These days his head swayed from side to side with the effort of movement, like it was on a kind of pivot between his shoulders. Getting old, I suppose.

"You know what I sometimes wish?"

"What's that, Gordon?" asked Colin.

"I know it's silly, but I sometimes wish that I could make time run backwards for a while."

"I know what you mean."

"To the moment when we were in the burger bar, just as Holloway was paying the waitress. Just that moment. And hold it there so everything would be left exactly as it was. Sort of preserved."

"I'm not sure about that, Gordon," Colin said. "If you froze that moment you wouldn't be able to experience this one, would you? And nor would I for that matter."

"I suppose you're right."

"I usually am."

Out of the distance a cyclist was coming along the river bank towards us and I pulled Colin to heel and edged to the side of the path, holding on to his collar until it had passed. The bike didn't pass, though. There was a squeak of wet brakes and a figure in a blue cagoule stepped off the pedals and stood beside us. It was Claire.

"Hello," she said.

She bent down to rub Colin behind the ears. Her hood was pulled into a tight, blue frame round her face and her cheeks were shiny from cycling into the drizzle. She looked well. Very well. I told her so.

"Yes, I feel OK," she said, still kneeling by Colin and stroking his head.

It was the first time I'd seen her since the change of school. And here she was making a big fuss of Colin, not me. I wouldn't have minded having my head stroked a bit. Maybe I should've been a dog. Still, I didn't blame her. I guessed she was feeling a bit awkward. And she had stopped. She could've cycled by and pretended not to notice. That has happened with a few people from the old place. Notably Brains.

She stood up and looked me in the eye.

"I ... I haven't been in touch," she said. "I'm sorry."

"Don't worry about it."

"I wasn't too well."

"I know."

Nervous exhaustion they called it. She didn't return to school after the day of the race. I wondered how long all that had been building up inside her. And, of course, I felt sick about it. Felt I was partly to blame. Holloway made it pretty clear that he did too. And he warned me off going to see her.

"Still," I said, "you look fine now. As I said."

"I could've done something to help, Gordon. No one told me what was happening to you."

"Honestly, it's all right. I'm probably better off where I am."

"St Peter's?"

"Yes. It's OK. They leave me alone. A few of the staff give me funny looks, as if they expect me to start foaming at the mouth or something. But I don't give trouble."

"I don't know," she said with a little frown. "You look sort of ... trodden in. Very quiet."

"I wasn't very noisy before," I said.

She pulled her hood off and shook her hair, still frowning.

"But you're all right?"

"I'm fine," I said. "Really."

"We should have a talk some time. A proper talk. If you like, that is."

"Yes, I would like that. Maybe we could have a burger or something. One each this time."

Colin and I watched her cycle off till she was almost out of sight. She wobbled a little as she turned to wave.